THE TITANIC LEGACY

BOOK THREE OF THE HUNTER FILES

ROB JONES

First published in 2021. This edition published in Great Britain in 2025 by Boldwood Books Ltd.

Copyright © Rob Jones, 2021

Cover Design by Tom Sanderson

Cover Images: Adobe Stock and Shutterstock

The moral right of Rob Jones to be identified as the author of this work has been asserted in accordance with the Copyright, Designs and Patents Act 1988.

All rights reserved. No part of this book may be reproduced in any form or by any electronic or mechanical means, including information storage and retrieval systems, without written permission from the author, except for the use of brief quotations in a book review. This book is a work of fiction and, except in the case of historical fact, any resemblance to actual persons, living or dead, is purely coincidental.

Every effort has been made to obtain the necessary permissions with reference to copyright material, both illustrative and quoted. We apologise for any omissions in this respect and will be pleased to make the appropriate acknowledgements in any future edition.

A CIP catalogue record for this book is available from the British Library.

Paperback ISBN 978-1-80600-017-3

Large Print ISBN 978-1-80600-016-6

Hardback ISBN 978-1-80600-015-9

Trade Paperback ISBN 978-1-80635-343-9

Ebook ISBN 978-1-80600-018-0

Kindle ISBN 978-1-80600-019-7

Audio CD ISBN 978-1-80600-010-4

MP3 CD ISBN 978-1-80600-011-1

Digital audio download ISBN 978-1-80600-014-2

This book is printed on certified sustainable paper. Boldwood Books is dedicated to putting sustainability at the heart of our business. For more information please visit https://www.boldwoodbooks.com/about-us/sustainability/

Boldwood Books Ltd, 23 Bowerdean Street, London, SW6 3TN

www.boldwoodbooks.com

For my children, at the very start of their adventure

1

10 APRIL 1912

The two thieves ran like the wind, weaving in and out of the busy crowd to evade their hunter, as they had done so many times before.

But this time was very different. Usually, they made off with no more than the contents of a picked pocket or a snatched purse. A handful of florins, some silver shillings, or perhaps a lady's watch or her precious golden rings. One time in Marylebone, they'd knocked the hat off a policeman and vanished into the fog with it, just for kicks. They left the world-famous custodian's helmet atop a bollard just for fun. All these things were easy to run with and even easier to fence, but while part of today's new treasure was a simple gold and emerald ring inscribed with some strange symbols, the other part was something neither of them had ever even heard of before, never mind seen or held in their hands.

A small golden idol, smooth and yellow and strangely unsettling to look at, all packed away in a canvas bag slung over Jeremiah's shoulder.

Neither thief knew what it was, but the robbery in which they had stolen it, just like this chase, was thrilling and exhilarating and dangerous, and young Jeremiah Brown had never felt more alive. The pickpocket from south London darted in between a young couple, parting them with his hands as he sprinted through the excited crowd. Ahead of him, his partner in crime was struggling to keep up. But George Wood, from the foggy wharves and dark alleys of the Isle of Dogs, looked like he was enjoying himself every bit as much as his friend from south of the river.

"Urry up, Georgie, you silly bastard!' Jeremiah cried out over his shoulder. 'He's almost close enough to grab your shirt tails!'

The young thief turned and laughed, not a care in the world. 'The devil will catch me first!'

They ran to a crossroads and turned into another street. There, at the far end of the narrow road, they saw a small section of the ship, moored up in Southampton dock on this cool, English spring morning.

'Bloody 'ell! Will you look at that! Look at the size of her!'

George skidded to a halt beside his friend, heart pounding in his chest. When he stared up at the enormous passenger ship at the end of the road, he almost forgot to breathe. 'I ain't never seen nothing like it, Jez. Imagine what she looks like inside!'

Behind them, they heard the private investigator screaming again. 'Stop those two boys!'

Jeremiah and George looked at each other, the smiles of awe and amazement on their young, filthy faces quickly fading. 'In that case, we'd better get a bloody move on, or we'll never find out!' With that, Jeremiah was gone, fleet-footed as he made his way down the rest of the street towards the giant passenger ship.

George, still standing on the pavement, turned and saw Luther Dankworth bearing down on him, black Homburg hat gripped in his right hand as he ran. His old friend was almost at the end of the street now, the stolen goods tucked safely inside his canvas bag.

'Wait for me, Jez!'

George took off, running down the street towards the mighty transatlantic liner. When he turned the corner, he saw hundreds of people bustling everywhere. Above them, black smoke was drifting from the massive ship's front three smokestacks as people climbed the gangways and boarded her. Jeremiah had told him back in London on the morning of the robbery that the fourth stack was a fake, built just to make the ship look bigger. He'd laughed at him, but now he knew his old friend was right again, just as normal.

'Get a move on, Georgie!'

Much younger and fitter, the two boys weaved through the crowd and put some distance between themselves and Dankworth. He had been on their tail since the robbery back in London a few days earlier, but it was time to say goodbye to him. Slipping out of sight in the bustling throng, George followed Jeremiah as he moved away from the ship and headed back towards the next road along. It was a feint. When they reached the corner of the road, they knocked over a woman and caused a gasp of horror. A man shouted and waved his fist at the two boys, but the job was done and they double-backed on themselves.

Dankworth had seen the hubbub and turned in its direction. At the same time, the two boys slipped once again out of sight and reversed course, using a large stack of crates holding bottled beer for cover. Like several other mountains of crates holding lemons, limes, oranges, vegetables, and meat and eggs, the beer was slowly being loaded inside the great ship's cargo hold. Jeremiah was no slouch and had clocked the crates as soon as he turned onto Berth 44. Now, he led George behind the piles of food and other cargo. Nearly half a million dollars' worth, he'd read in *The Times*. Everything from cotton to orchids, perfume to tennis balls. It was all going into the enormous hold for the long maiden journey across the Atlantic.

And so were Jeremiah and George, but not in the cargo hold. The two young Londoners had a cheap third-class cabin in steerage waiting for them just as soon as they could get there. Someone made a joke in the crowd and everyone laughed. Behind them, Dankworth was already lost in the throng, halfway across the berth to the water on the other side. The atmosphere was electric. Still on the move, Jeremiah reached into his pocket and pulled out a small piece of straw-coloured paper. George did the same, and they slowed to a walk before reaching the end of the remaining cargo still waiting to go on board.

'Take a look at that,' Jeremiah said, looking at his ticket. 'Third Class. White Star Line. Royal and United States Mail Steamers. It's all here, Georgie. Third Class Steerage Passenger's Contract Ticket. Our ticket to a new life.' He gave a loud, heartfelt laugh. 'My deepest and most sincere thanks to Ismay, Imrie & Co of Cockspur Street, London!'

The more cautious George looked behind him, but no sign of Dankworth. As they made their way towards the third-class boarding gangways down on the dock, he grew even more excited and stared at the date stamped on his ticket with elation. 'The tenth of April 1912, Jez. That new life starts today.'

Jeremiah looked up above and watched the cranes hoisting baggage up onto the ship and second-class passengers boarding on elevated gangways leading them to the higher decks, his smile fading. 'And next time we sail, we'll be in first class, not even second class. Penniless immigrants one day, and millionaires the next. Talking of which, we'd better go and speak to our man, Georgie. Get the ball rolling. Get our wages for a good job done.'

Inside the steerage area, Jeremiah found it harder than he'd imagined to make his way up to the agreed meeting place on the promenade deck. As third-class ticket holders, their outside access was largely restricted to the poop deck at the stern and the fore and aft well decks. But after a few short spells in Millbank and Holloway prisons, Jeremiah was unimpressed by the ship's security and found it wanting. After vaulting a few rails and ducking behind some lifeboats, he was able to successfully lead his friend to the appointment with their employer.

And there he was. George nudged Jeremiah with his elbow. 'Looks like the Grim Reaper.'

Jeremiah chuckled. 'In which case, I hope your soul is ready for heaven, my friend. I know mine ain't.'

'And who's that behind him?' George pointed to a large man dressed in a cheap brown suit. He had a chest like a Chianina bull and a thick black moustache, and he loitered a few yards away from the bench, hands behind his back.

'Maybe one of his thugs,' Jeremiah said. 'Be careful. Just wait here a second, me old mate.'

George waited nervously as his old friend disappeared from sight for a few moments. When he returned, he was straightening his jacket and taking the bag from his shoulder.

'Right then, Georgie. Let's do it. Oh, and just agree with whatever I say.'

They approached the man. He was the sole user of a long wooden bench, situated at the stern end of the second-class promenade deck. From his clothes alone, Jeremiah and George both knew he'd walked down from first class to meet them halfway. He looked up, saw them, checked a gold pocket watch, and then rose to greet them. A smile was nowhere to be seen on his thin, white face.

'Brown and Wood?'

A strange accent, Jeremiah thought. Maybe German.

'That's us, sir.'

'You have fulfilled the contract?'

A loud, deep horn emanated above them and filled the docks. Frightened seagulls took to the air. 'We have, sir.'

He sighed and stared out to sea. 'Then where are they?'

'They, sir?'

He turned to them, his face forming into a hard, sly leer. Sunken cheeks partially obscured by impressive sideboards of silvery hair. Thin, hateful lips. Eyes shaded by the brim of an expensive, impeccable black silk top hat. In his right hand, a beautiful walking cane of Zebrano wood with a solid brass handle, cast into the shape of a spitting cobra's open mouth.

'The ring and the idol, boy. Where are they?'

'Ah, well, that's just it, sir. See, we had a bit of a problem back in London.'

The eyes grew smaller and colder. 'Problem?'

'Yeah, didn't we, George?'

He nudged George in the ribs and his confused friend quickly nodded in agreement. 'Yes, sir. A problem.'

'Explain.'

'We got to the 'ouse you told us about. The address was right an' all, but inside we only found the ring. No idol.'

The man growled. 'Don't lie to me, you little wretch. I already read in the newspapers about the robbery. Both the ring and the idol were taken.'

'I swear, sir! It's not a lie. There was no idol. We read that too. Old Skulberg's lying just so's he can get his 'ands on the insurance. I swear it up and down, sir. On me mother's life.'

'It's true!' George said. 'We couldn't believe it when we read it, sir.'

After a long pause, the old man said, 'And the ring?'

Jeremiah produced a small purple velvet box with a smile. 'Here, sir.'

The man snatched the box, opened it, and regarded the small golden ring for a few seconds. Shining yellow metal and sparkling green emerald. Captivating in its beauty. When his eyes fell on the strange carvings, he smiled briefly and snapped the box shut, pocketing it in his suit.

'And there was definitely no idol with this ring?'

'Not in the whole place, sir. We trashed it good and proper.'

He raised an eyebrow. 'I read about that in the paper too.'

'And there was no idol, I swear it!' Jeremiah said.

'It's possible, I suppose. Konrad, search them both.'

The enormous man in the brown suit stepped forward, grabbed a fistful of each boy's jacket with each hand, and dragged them to the side of the promenade deck.

'You won't find it,' Jeremiah protested. 'Because we ain't got it!'

The old man smiled a thin, hateful smile. 'Nonetheless.'

After the search, the old man ordered Konrad to step away. Then he walked over to them both, slowly and with menace. As he peered down at them, he frowned hard. His gaze was icy and cold and seemed to bore into their very souls. 'And you say that you couldn't find the idol anywhere in Skulberg's mansion?'

'No, sir,' Jeremiah said. The earlier confidence he had felt back on the dock was rapidly fading away in the man's sombre presence. 'Not anywhere, sir. Just like we said.'

'And you are sure you looked everywhere?'

'Even in the cellar, sir,' George said. 'Just like you told us to.'

The tall man in the black top hat sighed impatiently, his stare hardening further. A brisk wind from the northwest whipped across the deck and cut the temperature on an already cool day. 'If you are lying to me, I'll have Konrad slit your throats. Think very carefully about what you are telling me. I am not a man to be trifled with. Professor Ernst Bauer is a name that strikes fear in many men much more fearless than you two wastrels, believe me.'

Jeremiah wondered if that were true. Remembering he was a seasoned thief from the rough end of London and this man was no more than a stuffed shirt who looked about a hundred years old, Jeremiah decided to change tack. Narrowing his eyes, he closed in on Bauer and lowered his voice. 'If we'd found it, you'd be 'olding it in them soft little 'ands of yours, wouldn't you now, Prof? Unless you're doubting the veracity of my word, that is, guvnor.'

A gamble, to be sure, but one that paid off. Bauer lifted his chin and took a step back. 'No, I accept your explanation. He must have moved it to another property and lied for insurance purposes. That's the sort of filthy trick he would do. Anyway, it's too late to worry about it now. Wherever it is, I will find it eventually. Here is the money I owe you for your work.'

He reached a long, white hand into his pocket and handed the two teenagers a handful of silver coins. 'Now, be off with you. Back to steerage where you belong. And don't try to intimidate me again or I'll have you arrested when we reach New York. Now, go.'

'Thankin' you kindly, sir!' Jeremiah said with a mock bow. 'And here's to 'opin' we never run into each other again. C'mon, Georgie! We've got a new world to discover. Let's leave this old fossil and get on with our lives!'

They made their way back to the forward well deck, stopping on the way to collect the wrapped-up idol from where Jeremiah had hidden it behind the number two cargo hatch when he'd momentarily left George on his own. Then Jeremiah pulled a bottle of brandy from his bag and cracked it open.

'Maybe we should have just handed it over, Jez,' George said, swigging from the bottle of brandy and wiping his mouth roughly with the sleeve of his jacket. 'I mean, what if the old bastard never believed us and searches the ship? What if he has the coppers waiting for us in New York?'

Jeremiah weighed the golden idol in his hand, admiring the way it sparkled in the sunlight, staring at the strange letters, like Greek but different. He laughed. 'You know what your problem is, don't you, Georgie? You worry too much! What if this, what if that, what if the other... You can worry about anything. Here – give us that bottle, you're 'oggin' it.'

He snatched the brandy from his younger friend and took a long, deep swig. When he'd finished draining half an inch off the top, he smacked his lips, held the bottle at arm's length, and stared out at the cold sea. 'We're going to be rich, Georgie! Rich as dukes! When we get to America, we'll sell this thing and pocket the cash. Buy us a business. Make us rich, rich, rich!'

George began to relax. 'You think?'

'Course I do! Whatever this thing is, it's got to be worth more than a fistful of silver. That old bastard must think we were born yesterday. Who the hell hands over a piece of gold as heavy as this for a handful of silver coins? Not me. I didn't come down with the last bloody shower. That grubby little ring, maybe. It was still gold, but there weren't enough of it to melt down into a single gold sovereign, was there now?' He tapped the side of George's head. 'Think about it! Maybe that little green gem was worth something more, but I don't care. Besides, we needed to give the old sod something or he'd have been too suspicious. So get rid of the ring and keep this beautiful golden statue all for us. Think about it!'

The ship sounded its loud horn as tugs began to push its stern out into the dock. George sipped more brandy, his face growing more thoughtful as he looked at the golden idol in his friend's hands. 'So, now what?'

'Now, we set sail for America, Georgie. We set sail for America and an amazing new life.'

2

PRESENT DAY

Reynaldo Ferrari was a squat, broad man with a thirst for blood and a hunger for gold. Raised in the Argentinian Highlands, he was as hard as a rock and twice as ugly. He knew from years of street fighting that the first punch was always the hardest and getting in hard and fast mattered the most. He was no believer in finesse, just force. After all, there was always a bigger fish. He once killed a man with one bare-knuckle strike to the head, for no reason at all. In the quiet moments, he told anyone who would listen that nurture did this to him, not nature, but not even he was completely certain of this.

He dragged on a cigarette as he watched the twilight fade and the neon world far below him quickly come to life. From their position high on Frenchman Mountain, Sin City was every bit as impressive as people had told him, but he wasn't here to debauch himself; far from it. A very serious man had told him he was here on the trail of the world's greatest secret.

'The world's greatest secret?' he'd asked the man. 'What sort of secret?'

'Nothing you need to worry about at this stage,' the man had said anxiously. 'Just do as you are told and you'll find out everything when the time is right.'

Ferrari did not believe this man. He knew how to read eyes and listen to the sound of a voice, its timbre and pitch. All much more important than listening to anyone's words, he had learned a long time ago. This man's eyes and voice told him that after he'd done as he was told, it was unlikely he would find out everything when the time was right. But that was a matter for later. Some accounts took longer to settle than others, after all.

Leaning on the side of a black GMC van covered in desert dust and chip marks, he inhaled more of the fragrant, hot smoke and watched the last of the sun slipping towards the horizon. Night had come to Nevada at last. He stopped slouching against the truck and told his men to get ready. Some of them were already in the truck, smoking. Others were outside on the trail, sitting on boulders and watching the sparkling lights of Las Vegas, far below. All five of them would soon be executing one of the most audacious heists in the state's history. For this gang of old thieves and jailbirds, it was the most important job any of them had ever done, and also the last. The man they were working for had told them failure was not an option. By the look on his face, he believed him. Ferrari saw that in his eyes, too.

'When is it time to get out of here?' Axelrod asked. He was one of the men looking out over the city. When he spoke, his cigarette bobbed up and down on his lips. 'I can't stand all this hanging around, boss. It's bad for my heart.'

Ferrari looked over at him. Like the others here, Axelrod had worked with him on countless jobs in Mexico and the US and was a solid member of the gang, even though he was known to have a very short and explosive temper.

'We wait until the planned time, old friend.' Ferrari wandered over to Axelrod, his snakeskin boots crunching on the gravel as he went. Flicking the burned-out cigarette stub from his hand, he immediately lit another cigarette and took a deep breath. 'There's no need to rush tonight, amigo. This is our last job together. After this, I never need to see your ugly face ever again.'

Axelrod chuckled. 'Or the faces of any of these other ugly bastards. I thought the same thing.'

One of the other men, a weightlifter from Yonkers called Tucker, said, 'Why couldn't we just wait for the bastards down on the road?'

'Yeah, we have the GPS tracker,' said Patterson, the man next to him. 'We can just wait for them to turn up. Easy as snapping a chick's neck.'

Carter, the last of the crew, a lean and worn Alaskan with skin like a cheap wallet, rolled his eyes.

'Because,' Ferrari said patiently, 'the tracker only allows us to track them. It does not tell us if they have arranged any kind of escort. To know this, we must use our eyes, like the hawk circling above your fat head.'

Carter scowled but calmed himself. 'If you say so.'

'Yeah, I say so,' Ferrari said, turning to Axelrod and lowering his voice back to its usual cool, controlled level. 'Tell me, what will you do with the money?'

'Donna wants to move to Palm Springs.' Axelrod's lips turned down at the corners of his mouth.

'Donna wants to move to Palm Springs?' Ferrari asked.

Axelrod nodded. 'Yeah. She wants to live in Palm Springs. She says the air is better for her health. Something about low humidity.'

'No good?'

'You know how I feel about surfing, boss. Sunset Beach, Oahu is where this old thief is spending his last few days.' He jabbed a fat thumb in the middle of his chest to underline the sentiment. This was happening, no matter what. Oahu. Donna would have to suck it up.

Ferrari laughed. 'I know you and I know Donna.'

Axelrod turned, cigarette still on his lip. 'And?'

'And I hope you enjoy your retirement in Palm Springs.'

Axelrod sighed. 'Yeah.'

Ferrari's eyes drifted from his old friend and danced over the Vegas skyline until they located the Luxor Las Vegas. With its twin ziggurat towers and Sphinx and steel-and-glass pyramid, the thirty-storey hotel and casino made up one of the most famous complexes in the world. It was beautiful, too. The way the neon reflected off the pyramid caught Ferrari's imagination. Sparked up something wicked in the darkness behind his eyes.

He thought maybe he'd like to blow a few hundred thousand dollars in there one day when the heat had died down. When he was free, a bird finally out of its cage. But it wouldn't be wise to go back for a very long time after knocking the place off. He was distracted for a few seconds by the last rays of sunshine striking the tops of the golden Mandalay Bay hotel towers, but then it was gone and his mind went back to the Luxor.

And one of the weirdest heists he had ever planned.

Ferrari had not been raised a thief, but a farmer. Life was hard on his father's farm in the Puna, and he'd moved to the city as soon as he was old enough to rent a hotel room. He'd had lofty dreams of starting a business and sending money back to his struggling parents, but Buenos Aires had other ideas. In less than a year he'd joined a gang and started robbing banks. His keen intelligence and meticulous planning soon elevated him to the very top of the pecking order in the city of tango's filthy underbelly.

Years passed. He grew richer, but his father knew where the money came from and refused it in the same way he refused to speak to his son while he was working as a common thief. When his parents died, he sold the farm for a pittance and never looked back. By then, he'd grown used to a life of speed and danger and easy money. His heart had grown as cold as ice. Remembering his father toiling in the fields evoked not pity but contempt. He was ashamed of his weakness and vowed never to let himself be brought so low. Honest work was meaningless unless it paid good money.

The hot desert air stirred his raven-black hair and pulled him from his thoughts, right back to the strange mission and the even stranger man who had ordered the job. Ferrari was no fool, and he knew that the man, who had called himself Scipio, had been very sparing with the mission's full details. All he knew, for now, was that the Luxor Las Vegas had a large exhibition of artifacts and other items of interest relating to the Titanic and that one of the items on show was an old, battered compass from the sixteenth century. Scipio had ordered him to acquire it.

Scipio had provided a handful of pictures of the object in question. This was how he knew what it looked like, and it looked like a piece of junk. It was gold though, but the money Scipio was paying them to liberate it from the exhibition was fifty times more than its metal value, and this got Ferrari thinking. Obviously, Scipio and his puppet-masters wanted the compass, not for its gold value, but for another reason. He doubted this reason was historical interest or to add to another collection somewhere. Just something about the way Scipio had talked gave him the impression he was no antiquities collector, and this made him suspicious. Whetted his thief's appetite.

No, they wanted the compass for another reason altogether, and whatever it was had to mean it was worth a hell of a lot more money than either its historical or metal value. The wily thief from Argentina had spent a lot of time wondering exactly just what this might be, but despite some colourful speculation, he'd come up mostly blank. There was obviously something special and unique about this particular compass beyond its association with the *Titanic*, but it was impossible to know what it was. A secret message? Something built into it, to make it give different directions to some special place? There was only one way to find out, and that was to get a better look at it. Luckily, that was exactly what Scipio was paying him to do.

After sweeping Sin City one more time with his binoculars, Ferrari closed in on the Luxor Las Vegas and saw what he had been waiting for. A team of security guards was loading part of the exhibition into the back of an armoured truck parked outside the hotel complex. It was not a heavy load – just a handful of boxes containing certain treasures amassed over the years by a wealthy investor named Morton Woolf. Tonight, the exhibition was coming to an end and Mr Woolf was taking redelivery of his goods, including the compass.

Or so he thought.

'It's time, friends,' Ferrari said. 'Masks on, guns ready.'

3

With the balaclavas now joining the rest of their black combat fatigues and automatic weapons, the small group had silently transformed from a team of thieves to a unit of paramilitary soldiers, minutes out from the mission of their lives. As darkness gathered over Frenchman Mountain, the armoured truck full of the loot trundled out of the city's eastern districts and joined Las Vegas Boulevard North, cruising past the airport and snaking up towards the Valley of Fire State Park.

Ferrari ordered the men into the van and took one more look at the map on his phone, zooming in on the armoured truck's present location, indicated to him thanks to a GPS tracker Axelrod had installed earlier in the day. Then he swiped across to where the action was going down, on a small desert track leading up to the Woolf property just a few short miles away.

The notion of raiding the property itself for the compass after delivery had easily been dismissed. Woolf was one of America's richest men, and his Nevada desert compound made Fort Knox look like a gingerbread house. That was part of the issue with knocking off the Luxor Las Vegas, too. The hotel complex had some of the heaviest private security in the country. No, there was only one way to strike and be sure of success. A smash and grab out on the highway, in the grand old tradition.

'Are we ready, my old friend?'

Ferrari looked up. Axelrod had paused on his way into the van. Most of his face was hidden by the mask, but his eyes were clear enough.

'Yeah, we're ready.'

'What about them?' Axelrod flicked his head to indicate the others inside the van.

'They'll find out soon enough.'

Axelrod smirked. 'I guess so.'

It was crazy, but Ferrari felt a twinge of guilt. It was easily shaken off. He climbed into the van beside his old friend and fired up the engine. 'We have a short drive to the position and then things will move fast. Everyone go through the plan in their heads one more time. If heaven is your thing, then say your prayers. Woolf's guards are all former Special Forces.'

They pulled away, gravel crunching under the chunky Vandura tyres. Turning off the track that led up to the ridge they had parked on, they now made their way off the mountain and down to the rendezvous. For a while, they cruised on the Valley of Fire Highway. They smoked cigarettes and told a couple of blue jokes. When they reached the unsealed track leading into the Woolf property, they pulled off onto it and climbed out of the van.

Ferrari asked, 'Everyone have their weapons?'

Nods.

'Then tip her over.'

Carter hauled the jack out of the back of the van. It was an electric power jack and soon had the GMC tipped up at forty degrees in the middle of the track. Without speaking, the five men now rocked the van until it crashed down on its side, totally blocking the track.

'Into positions.'

They scattered behind boulders and mesquite trees, ducked down low and out of sight. Guns in hand, they waited in silence. The only light was that of the bright full moon over their heads, a dazzling white disc in the star-studded black void stretching to infinity high over the desert. Ferrari consulted his smartphone.

'They're almost here.'

Phone back in his pocket and gun at the ready, he searched for a visual on the armoured car. He didn't have to wait long. Headlights swept in an arc across the desert night as the armoured truck pulled off the highway and turned into the track leading down to the Woolf compound. Then they saw the upturned GMC and pulled to a stop. The engine idled in the darkness. The guard in the passenger seat was already on the radio.

'Go, go, go!' Ferrari said.

The men stormed the truck, Carter and Patterson from the east, Ferrari and Tucker from the west. Axelrod was at the rear, placing explosives on the rear doors. The men inside wound their windows and opened fire. Ferrari's men returned fire, never stopping their advance on the vehicle. Axelrod finished the placement of the explosive and ran around to the side, hitting the detonator and blowing the back doors off. A burning man stumbled out of the back, screaming in agony as the flames licked over his body.

Ferrari peppered him with rounds and ended the pain. Carter and Tucker raked dozens of bullets into the guards at the front, biting and chipping and tearing at the open windows and blasting broken glass into their bullet-pocked faces. As they slumped dead inside, Carter and Tucker reached into the truck on either side and opened the doors, dragging the two corpses out and across the sand away from the vehicle.

Ferrari looked at his watch as he ran to the back of the truck. Clockwork. He and Axelrod checked the boxes were in place. Then Axelrod reached under the rear fender and grabbed the magnetic GPS tracker, tossing it out onto the sand. There was another one belonging to the company somewhere, but that wouldn't be a problem for long. They climbed inside, Patterson joining them. Tucker was at the wheel with Carter beside him. They reversed the truck and spun around in a tight half-circle, flicking up a great arc of sand and grit. Then they took off with a wheel-spinning roar, reaching the end of the track and turning right onto the Valley of Fire Highway.

After a short drive, they pulled off the highway at Elephant Rock and unloaded the exhibition crates into an old Winnebago with fake Utah plates. Then they torched the armoured truck and walked over to their new vehicle.

'Why don't we just keep it ourselves?' Tucker said.

'Yeah. I read online it's worth five million bucks,' Carter said. 'That's one mill each.'

'It's worth a hell of a lot more than that,' Ferrari said.

Tucker and Patterson turned to face him. Tucker said, 'You think?'

'I most certainly do, maybe a hundred million, or more. Something tells me that in this case, the sky's the limit.'

Patterson was running the figures in his head. A light went on. 'That's twenty million dollars each! Holy cow.'

Ferrari and Axelrod laughed.

'No, amigo,' Ferrari said. 'Your math is off. It's fifty million dollars each.'

'Wait, what?' said Tucker. 'One hundred million divided by five is twenty million.'

'But divided by two it's fifty million,' Ferrari said, his smile fading.

'I don't get it,' Patterson said.

Carter was a step ahead of him and reached for his gun. He was too late. Axelrod opened fire with an M5, slashing the three men to ribbons of bloodied flesh and shredded guts. They never even had a chance to work out it was the end of the trail.

'Good work, amigo,' Ferrari said, patting his old partner on the back.

They searched for the compass and found it, dumping the rest of the exhibits in their crates a few yards from the burning truck.

Ferrari said, 'Maybe with fifty million, you can persuade Donna to move to the beach after all. That much might get you a half-decent beach house in Malibu.'

Axelrod laughed as the two men climbed inside the Winnebago. 'Maybe, maybe.'

Ferrari smiled as he turned the Winnebago onto the highway and headed west, back towards Las Vegas. The way he figured it, state troopers would be looking for people leaving the area, not driving into it. And no one was finding the compass, as soon it would be buried deep inside the steering wheel's airbag module.

'We're almost there, old friend,' he said. 'We deliver this to Scipio and maybe we might find out what's going on.'

'Maybe, maybe.'

Ferrari wondered why Scipio induced the same doubt and wariness in his old friend that he did in him. He just hoped the treasure at the end of this trail would be worth all the trouble. Something told him it just might be.

4

Max Hunter rolled back the bedcovers and yawned. It was still dark outside his Washington apartment and when he checked the time, he saw why. The clock on the bedside table delivered the grim news that it was just before five o'clock in the morning. Worse, he knew there was no hope of getting back to sleep. His mind was chock-full of thoughts and concerns.

First up was his career. He was enjoying life in the HARPA team, but he still found himself thinking about his previous incarnation working as the lead field archaeologist for UNESCO. He had worked hard to achieve such a senior and demanding position, climbing rungs on a steep ladder, starting as an officer in the British Army's highly respected Grenadier Guards. From there, life had taken an interesting twist and he found himself writing an archaeology doctorate at the University of Oxford. After just a few months lecturing and researching for Carmarthen College, Oxford, he was poached by Professor Juliette Bonnaire and invited to work for UNESCO in Paris.

C'est la vie.

His work there was complicated and sensitive and sometimes political; working in such a senior role at the United Nation's main agency for cultural and natural heritage could never be anything but this. He'd felt it was a natural progression for his career, possibly leading one day right into Juliette's office, but then destiny's sleight of hand had pulled another fast one and threw him into the warm arms of Agent Amy Fox in Washington DC.

That was life, he guessed.

And life was good. He and Amy hadn't exactly hit it off right from the start, but by the end of their first job together things were different. He liked her. Maybe a little more than like. In fact, he was sure of it. He liked his new job, too. HARPA, the Heritage, Artifacts, and Relics Protection Agency, had been established as a subsidiary division of the FBI after he and Amy and the rest of their small team had discovered and secured the site of Atlantis. Led by the highly decorated former US naval officer, Director James Gates, it offered a chance for Hunter to relive some of the excitement he'd experienced as a younger man in the military and offered the supplemental benefit of working alongside some really great people whom he already counted as good friends.

So why was he up at night worrying about if he should have stayed at UNESCO? He yawned again and rolled over, crushing back down into the sheets and giving sleep one more shot. No answers would come at this time of the morning, and he had to attend a Gates briefing at nine, sharp, so he wanted to be at his best. He knew it was something about the *Titanic* – Gates had hinted that on their flight back to the US from Turkey yesterday. So far, so good, but he was having trouble thinking about what this could mean. The *Titanic* had sunk over one hundred years ago, after all.

And now he was wide awake again.

* * *

Amy Fox was sipping her third cup of freshly ground coffee in her favourite reading chair. Even though it was dark outside, and she was exhausted from the demanding and dangerous mission they had just finished, she too was finding it hard to sleep. Exhaustion always did that to her. She was just one of those people. The more tired she felt, the harder it was to get good sleep, but Amy being Amy, she decided to put the time to good use. Sitting in the low light of a little Tiffany lamp given as a birthday gift by her mother, she was secretly hoping Gates's cryptic mention of the *Titanic* would come to nothing. She could use a few days doing nothing, that was for sure.

Her phone buzzed on the side table. She looked down at the screen and sighed – James Gates.

Talk of the devil and he's sure to appear.

Or in this case, merely thinking of the devil, she thought. That wasn't fair. Gates was one of the nicest and most generous professionals she had ever worked with. He was fair, kind, and efficient and he worked hard. Damned hard, and that was why he was texting her at this time in the morning. The few words at the start of the message simply read: *Get up, get coffee, get here*, followed by a small winking emoji.

She couldn't resist the corners of her mouth turning up slightly, partly from seeing the typically brief and to-the-point Gates text, but mostly because he'd finally worked out how to use an emoji and taken the time to send her one. She'd been working on that for months. As far as the instructions in the short message went, she'd already managed to do parts one and two. She was up and she was drinking coffee. Now for part three – getting into the office.

She got out of the armchair and walked through her Georgetown apartment to the bedroom, passing a handful of family pictures on her way – Dad on a pier holding an impressive Spanish mackerel up to the camera, proud to have caught a rare visitor to Delaware waters; Mom playing her violin in the orchestra. So many memories, and so quick and easy to walk past, but her life was just moving too fast to stop and think about the important things.

She hated that.

As she got dressed, she switched from Apartment Amy to Office Amy. Her father taught her this little trick, how to compartmentalise her mind and retain the degree of sanity required to balance a job like hers with something resembling a private life worth living. Office Amy was a very different kettle of fish to Apartment Amy. Apartment Amy noticed things like how the cushion on her reading chair needed to be replaced, or that the coffee was nearly gone. She registered things like the scent of the perfume on her clothes or the beauty of a sunrise.

Office Amy never saw any of that.

Office Amy was all about the goal, the target, keeping on point, and her mind was already spinning up, ready for whatever Gates might be about to spring on her and the rest of Team HARPA. Sure, he'd mentioned the

Titanic, of which she knew very little, but beyond that, it could mean absolutely anything. After all, the first two HARPA missions had been totally different. The first had pitted her up against a strange Illuminati cult called The Creed and their crazed plans to obtain ancient and powerful weaponry from Atlantis.

Oh yeah, she'd also discovered Atlantis on the first mission.

She still couldn't believe it, but there had been no time for resting on her laurels. Fresh on the heels of that mission had come her doomed arrest of Alexis Kandarian and taking him into custody in a bid to stop him from destroying the world with his Revelation relic. Now, as she hurried out of the door and climbed into her car, she wondered exactly what Gates's latest operation would have in store for her. Whatever it was, she wouldn't have to wait long to find out.

Zipping through Georgetown before the rest of the city came to life, she found her mind drifting to the others in her team. She was their leader and it was her responsibility to make sure they were all up to the task ahead. Fundamentally, she knew they all were, but she was concerned by the lack of downtime they'd had since defeating Kandarian and returning from Turkey, which at this time could only be counted in hours.

The problem was, there was little any of them could do about it. Gates had spelled out the serious duties and responsibilities of HARPA when they'd formally established the agency, and she knew him well enough to know he'd cut anyone not up to it loose in a heartbeat. Nothing personal and no hard feelings. You'd still get a warm smile in the corridor and an invite to his famous Fourth of July barbecue, but you wouldn't be on board the team any more.

No deadwood, not ever, was how the big man had phrased it. She could still hear his voice saying it in her head. All good, she thought – at least as far as she was concerned. She was agency through and through. She guessed Lewis, the former US Marine, and brand-new dad, was a sure bet too, but her management side wasn't so sure when she thought about the others.

Quinn was a wild card. No one knew anything about 'Ghost', and she was unpredictable and unstable. On the one hand, Amy thought the young woman needed a family and HARPA provided that role, so she would stick around. On the other hand, it didn't take a vast leap of the imagination to visualise her getting bored and moving on. With Quinn Mosley, there was just no way to tell.

She cruised around Dupont Circle and exited on Massachusetts Avenue. The sun was still below the horizon but the cloudless sky in the southeast, directly ahead of her, was starting to brighten up with a faint pink blush. Mirror check and no cops around, she pushed down on the throttle and increased her speed, keen to get to the briefing before the rest of the team. As she settled back down into the soft leather seat, her mind returned to worrying about how long the original HARPA team would stay together.

If Quinn was hard to predict, Jodie was much easier. To the casual observer, Jodie looked like she'd probably be first to jump ship, but this would be misunderstanding the thief from California. Unlike Quinn, Jodie had opened up to Amy and talked to her about her family life and how HARPA was her new home. Amy knew she had nowhere else to go and was still running from some of the darker parts of her past. Amy was pretty damn sure Jodie Priest was staying the course.

Sal Blanco was harder. He was the team's rock, but he was older and sometimes after a few beers he let talk of retiring slip out into the conversation. Most days she half-expected his resignation from the team and there was nothing to do about that. She couldn't talk him out of it and wouldn't want to anyway. For now, she was just glad he was on board.

And then there was Hunter. The arrogant, cocky, smart-assed Englishman who seemed to think he was somewhere between Indiana Jones and James Bond. Problem was, he was as good as advertised. His military leadership experience was solid and respectable, and his academic archaeological knowledge second to none, with Oxford and UNESCO looming large on his resume. An even bigger problem was, she was falling in love with the bastard.

Damn it all.

5

Director James Gates removed his suit jacket and draped it over the back of a chair at the business end of Team HARPA's main conference room. Whistling as he shook a mouse on the table, bringing the computer to life, he opened a folder and clicked on one of the thumbnail images inside. Instantly, a large photograph of the *Titanic* appeared on the screen behind him.

The tall, lean man with short silver hair now rubbed his hands together, blew out a deep breath, and faced his team.

'As you know from my call, something big has come up.'

'Not unusual for this time in the morning,' Hunter said, yawning.

'Oh please,' Jodie said.

'Settle down, everyone,' Gates said. 'Including you, Dr Hunter. As I was saying, we could have a big problem – or at least, that's the speculation.'

'Sounds ominous,' Amy said.

'Or promising,' said Hunter, 'depending on your point of view and general outlook on life.'

Amy had turned to look at him to hear his contribution. Now she arched an eyebrow and showed him the back of her head. 'So, what's the story, Jim?'

Gates was smiling at the dynamic between his protégé and the Englishman, but the corners of his mouth soon fell back down again. 'The story starts with a phone call I got when you guys were still in Turkey a few days ago. It was from an old friend of mine, Olav Skulberg in Oslo, Norway. He's an old seadog like me. I knew him from various naval exercises conducted with the Royal Norwegian Navy in the Arctic Circle back during the Cold War.'

'That was before you were born, Jodie,' Hunter said with a smirk. 'I'll send you the Bluffer's Guide after the briefing.'

'Hey, let's trade,' she said without skipping a beat. 'I have the Bluffer's Guide to Being an Old Asshole.'

Hunter straightened his tie. 'I'm not that old. Anyway, I prefer the expression "well-worn".'

Gates's face grew sterner. 'That's enough, everyone. I don't care if you were born before, during, or after the Cold War. That's beside the point, which is that Olav and I have not spoken for many years so I was surprised to hear from him. I was even more surprised to hear that his wife, Trine, had passed away after a long illness. She was a great lady. Anyway, after her passing, Olav decided to start collecting artifacts from the *Titanic*, a lifelong interest of his.'

'Of many people,' Lewis said. 'My uncle is crazy about it.'

'Not as crazy as Olav, is my best guess,' Gates said. 'You need to understand that when I say old seadog, I mean that before his retirement, he rose to the rank of Rear Admiral and attained the position of Chief of the Navy.'

'Head of the entire Norwegian Navy?' Quinn asked.

Hunter said, 'When they make you Chief of the Navy, it's usually the whole thing and not just a little bit of it.'

'Bite me, Hunter,' Quinn said, but with a smile. 'I was just expressing my admiration for a man who had risen so high in the military. What was your rank again?'

'Major,' he said. 'A perfectly good rank. I even got a little crown on my rank insignia.'

'I'm sure that was very pretty,' Gates said, 'but around here officers wear stars.'

Jodie and Quinn high-fived, pleased with the rebuke, and after giving them a friendly wink, Gates continued his briefing. 'There's much more. Olav comes from a very wealthy oil family. Oil is as big in Norway as it is in Texas. When his parents died, he inherited a half-share, his sister up in

Trondheim getting the other half. He never told me how much, and I never asked, but I know it's in the ballpark of hundreds of millions of dollars, so when I say he started a collection, I mean he built a museum on the side of his mansion on an island just outside of Oslo. That museum now houses the third biggest collection of artifacts outside of the other main *Titanic* museums in Belfast, Northern Ireland, and Las Vegas, at the Luxor.'

Amy whistled. 'Whoa.'

'You got that right, Amy,' Gates said. 'He sent me some pictures and the place is like something out of the next century – all glass and steel and special lighting. It's also vast and filled not only with artifacts from the *Titanic* but also various educational items and interactive virtual reality experiences. Olav has impeccable taste and the entire museum is a very special place. He intends on opening it to the general public in a few months, but there's been a major hitch.'

'Let me guess,' Blanco said, the first contribution from the quiet man. 'This is where his phone call to you comes in?'

'Got it in one,' Gates continued. 'You see, Olav called me up to tell me that a few days ago, a team of thieves broke into his museum and stole one single exhibit from his museum.'

Hunter sat up and fixed his eyes on Gates, suddenly very interested in what the boss was saying. 'What sort of exhibit?'

'Ah, good to see you're paying attention, Dr Hunter,' Gates said with a grin. 'For a second there I was thinking about ordering someone to get you a pillow.'

'No need for that, Director Gates. I can sleep anywhere. Army training. It was the naval history of the Arctic Circle that did it. Better than sleeping pills. Thanks.'

'You're most welcome. But now, listen up and pay attention.'

'Yes, sir,' Hunter said with a mock salute.

Gates gave him a sideways glance and clicked on another thumbnail. A picture of a golden ring with a beautiful emerald appeared. Small, classy, nothing out of the ordinary. 'This is the object the thieves ransacked the museum for. It's all they took.'

Hunter frowned. 'Can I ask a question?'

'Be my guest.'

'Why did Admiral Skulberg simply not call the police about this robbery? Or did he?'

'He did not,' Gates said. 'And he was evasive about that when I asked him.'

'So, this was not a normal robbery, in other words?' Amy asked.

Gates shook his head. 'No, and that's why he contacted me. Since his wife's death, he tells me he's become almost a recluse, dedicating all of his time to the museum. He's already told me outright he won't be leaving the island under any circumstances. That's why he needs our help. He knows who I am and who you all are and what we do, or at least the parts of our work that are not classified. He even knew about both Max Hunter and his ego, which impressed me.'

'Me too,' Jodie said. 'I thought no one knew who you were, Hunter.'

'Thanks for your interest in my career,' Hunter said. 'If I'm ever interested in yours, I'll give you a call.'

As Jodie raised her middle finger, Gates resumed his talk with a sigh. 'Amy's right, as is usually the case around here. This was no ordinary robbery, and the reason Olav is so certain of this is for the simple reason that the thieves left significantly more expensive items behind while selecting this one single ring, something of much less value.'

'That tiny little ring was really all they took?' Lewis asked, pointing at the screen behind Gates.

The old man nodded, turned, and pointed at the picture with his pen. 'Right. That tiny little ring right there.'

'What's so special about it?' Blanco asked.

'Here, Olav grew evasive again, just as he had done when I asked him about the police. When I asked him about it, he kept his reply brief. Olav is not exactly loquacious, and during his phone call to me he was even less forthcoming than usual, but he told me he has a hell of a story to tell.'

'So, what's the plan?' Amy asked. 'When is he telling you this story?'

'Yeah, has he invited you over to his museum?' asked Jodie.

'Whether or not I ever get the chance to visit the Trine Skulberg Titanic Museum is up for grabs, but what is much more certain is that you all will. He's asked me to send my best team out to Oslo to see if they can work out who's behind the robbery and why they wanted to steal the ring. He's especially interested in Dr Hunter's expertise, having read all about the escapades at the Gates of Nineveh.'

'It's only natural he should seek out the best,' Hunter said.

'Luckily,' Jodie said, pointing her pen at the screen, 'that museum looks large enough to contain your ego while we're in Norway.'

'Yes,' Hunter said. 'That is lucky. But it's clearly not big enough to house your attitude.'

'Enough, please,' Gates said. 'This is a different kind of mission to what you're used to, and despite my friendship with Olav, I wouldn't sanction the visit if we were already working on another mission. But the fact is, Olav wouldn't have asked me if he didn't need serious help, and I know he's keeping a hell of a lot from me. It's your job to get that information out of him, especially if you're going to help him. Right now, we know only that they stole this ring.'

'Which is not much to go on,' Lewis said, twirling his pen.

'It's nothing at all,' said Gates with a frown.

Blanco's hand was wrapped around a mug of steaming black coffee. He lifted it to his lips and took a slow sip then set the mug back down on the table in his usual unrushed style. 'And that's really all we have?'

Gates paused. 'Yes and no. We also have this.'

Amy recognised a rare look of concern on her boss's usually calm face as he flicked onto the next image. It featured a man climbing into a metallic silver Maserati Levante. He was wearing a winter coat, black jeans, and a beanie. Recognising the face, Amy knew what came next. All eyes swivelled from the mugshot on the screen to the Max Hunter. They weren't disappointed with the reaction.

'Bugger me,' Hunter said, almost in a whisper. 'That's Brodie McCabe.'

6

'Brodie McCabe,' Gates said, repeating Hunter's astonishing words. 'Or as he likes to be known these days, Scipio, a reference to a Roman general.'

A hush fell over the briefing room.

'Where was this picture taken?' Amy asked.

Gates said, 'This image was taken by one of Olav's private security cameras fixed on the perimeter wall running around the museum.'

'And I guess I don't have to ask when it was taken,' Hunter said with a weary sigh.

'Minutes after the robbery.'

Hunter had felt an unexpected pang of nerves when he'd seen the face of his old nemesis flick up on the screen behind Gates. McCabe had once been an old friend in the army, but his bitter jealousy of Hunter had driven him into the heart of a vast secret society they now knew was called the Creed. He had been working for this underground network of reclusive elites, and against Hunter and the HARPA team, during the mission to discover Atlantis. Now, the obvious question was already forming on Hunter's lips.

'Are we to presume McCabe has stolen Skulberg's artifact on behalf of the Creed again?'

'I was kind of hoping you'd tell us,' said Gates. 'You know him better than anyone else here, and we have nothing else to go on except this picture. The licence plate on his car came to nothing. It was traced to a shell corporation registered in Estonia. Total dead end.'

Hunter stared at the image of his old friend up on the screen and considered the matter with care. The rest of the team were waiting for an answer, and he was keen not to let them, or himself, down with the reply. In the end, McCabe's furtive eyes gave him the information he needed.

'Yes, he's working for the Creed. Brodie was an average soldier and an even worse archaeologist with a penchant for plagiarising other colleagues' work and passing it off as his own. He even won an award for it once.'

'Sounds like a total asshole,' Blanco said. 'Sorry, Jim, but that just came out.'

'People like that always get what they deserve in the end,' said Jodie. 'I know he will, too.'

'I agree, and Sal's right too,' Hunter said. 'Brodie McCabe was and remains a total arsehole with a massive insecurity complex that makes him dangerous. He also has little idea of his limitations, believing himself to be right at the top of his game. But he was certainly no Indiana Jones. He was no good at working alone. He always needed someone to give him some direction, whether that was a senior officer in the regiment or a professor in his department, or out in the field. My money is firmly against Brodie McCabe's planning and executing a robbery, especially one of this nature, without significant direction by someone above. Brodie is a coward and a thief. Given his previous experience with the Creed, we should presume he's working for them and they're back on the scene.'

'Thanks, Max,' Gates said. 'I think that's a safe assumption but I wanted your view first.'

'But why would the Creed want an old ring from Olav's *Titanic* collection?' Amy asked.

'And not just a ring,' Gates said.

Lewis sat up straighter and lifted his chin, fixing his eyes on Gates. 'What does that mean? I thought you said Admiral Skulberg was perplexed because the gang had stolen only one item – the ring – and that this was odd because there are so many other things in the collection of far greater value?'

'I did, and it's good to know you were listening so closely.'

'Then, why say it wasn't just a ring they stole?' Quinn said. When everyone turned to her, she added, 'Hey, I listen too!'

'The answer is simple,' Gates said. 'Olav's museum was not the only place holding *Titanic* artifacts that got robbed. I called you in Turkey after Olav called me following the robbery at his museum, but in the last few hours I just found out that a part of the *Titanic* exhibition at the Luxor Las Vegas, a private collection on loan to the wider exhibition, was robbed on its way back to the owner, a certain Morton Woolf. The thieves stole a small sixteenth-century compass that was also once a passenger on board the ill-fated *Titanic*. Here, for your viewing pleasure, I have an image of it kindly provided by Mr Woolf's private office.'

He clicked his mouse and an official picture of the compass taken at the Luxor Las Vegas exhibition appeared behind him.

Instantly transfixed, the English archaeologist was up on his feet and walking over to the screen at the end of the room. 'Early to mid-sixteenth century, I'd say. Also, Spanish without a doubt.'

'I'm impressed,' Gates said. 'But then, that's why you're on this team.'

'It's beautiful,' Amy said.

Quinn yawned. 'Looks like a piece of worthless, dented old junk to me.'

'Which is why you stick to the technological stuff,' Amy said. 'Right, Max?'

He nodded. 'Right. It's certainly gold, for a start,' Hunter said. 'No tarnishing on the outside casing. Or mostly gold – the mechanical interior will be other harder-wearing metals. Easily worth at least thirty thousand dollars, and probably more because of its connection to the *Titanic*. And even more again if its provenance has anything interesting to offer beyond that. People pay a lot more at auction for an interesting story. Sometimes the story pushes the price up way more than the object's base value. Beyond the *Titanic*, do we know anything else about its life story or its original owner?'

'A little, but not much,' Gates said. 'Woolf, the owner, is a notorious recluse, but luckily the Luxor exhibition manager gave me some extra details in an email she sent just over an hour ago. The compass belonged to a colourful Spanish explorer named Francisco de Gama. He was born in 1490 to a very noble family in Brozas, Extremadura, a Spanish autonomous community on the Portuguese border. After a distinguished career in the military, he made a long expedition to the Americas in 1521, sailing from Spain on a fleet of over twenty ships. The fleet landed in the West Indies, but over time, de Gama made his way into Mexico and then further south.'

'A busy boy,' Amy said. 'What happened to him?'

'That's where it gets interesting because no one knows.' Gates clicked his mouse and changed the image on the screen from the compass to an oil painting of de Gama. The tall, slim man was wearing what looked like an expensive red silk shirt and some kind of blue sash. He stared back at them through the ageing oils, a look of exotic, knowing mystery captured deftly by the artist's skilled hand.

'No one knows, huh?' Quinn said.

'I like his beard,' said Jodie. 'Maybe you should grow one like that, Hunter?'

'I would, but I'm not sure you'd be able to control yourself around me if I did.'

She tipped her head back, a smirk on her lips. 'Yeah, right.'

'Can we get back to de Gama and his golden compass?' Blanco grumbled. 'I was starting to enjoy that.'

'There's not much to get back to, unfortunately,' Gates said. 'After returning to Spain following his adventures, Señor de Gama vanished without a trace. Some say he went back to the jungles of the New World; others say he travelled in Europe. No one knows his ultimate fate. We don't even know how his compass survived after whatever happened to him. Lauren Bryant over in Vegas, who manages the exhibition, has surmised that he was robbed and perhaps murdered, and that's how come the compass survived but not de Gama. We just don't know – yet.'

'But then, that's why we're gathered here at this ungodly hour, right?' Jodie asked.

Gates looked at his watch. 'Ungodly? It's almost eight in the morning. I don't understand.'

Jodie said, 'That little smirk on your face tells me you understand, all right.'

'The early bird gets the worm,' Gates said. 'And right now, that means I want to know why McCabe and the Creed are stealing objects from not one but two separate collections of *Titanic* artifacts. In my view, we must consider these two robberies linked. For one thing, Olav located the ring and the compass together back in the 1980s, so there's another link.'

'Where did he get them from?' Lewis asked.

'If I told you, you wouldn't believe it,' Gates said with a smile. 'I'll let him tell you that story. He's very proud of it. He's also unusually rattled, and I say that as someone who knows him well. And he's hiding something from me. I just know he is, and I want to know what it is. It won't be anything sinister. I trust him with my life, but I still want to know what it is. This means, when you're in Oslo, you have a lot of work to do.'

'When do we fly?' Amy asked.

'Call me presumptuous,' Gates said, 'but the HARPA jet you recently flew in from Turkey on is already fuelled, prepped with a flight plan to Oslo and waiting for the six of you over at Dulles.'

'Typical James Gates organisation,' Quinn said. 'Who could ask for more?'

'It's all good,' Blanco said. 'I hate long goodbyes.'

As they got up to leave, Gates called out to them, 'And one more thing. Make sure you show Olav the greatest of respect. He's got contacts at the very top level of the Norwegian military and government and more than that, he's my friend. As I say, I trust him with my life, and maybe he's putting his life in our hands, too.'

7

As the government jet cruised high above the Atlantic, Hunter's mind was still buzzing with the news of Brodie McCabe's involvement in the *Titanic* artifact thefts. The last time he saw McCabe it had been through the sights of a gun. After a brutal and bloody battle at the Atlantis site in eastern Greenland, McCabe and the Creed's team had tried to kill them all, deep inside the icy city. Hunter had replied in kind and fired at McCabe as he fled the battlefield, but he had missed and his nemesis fled the battle.

Hunter had been left with nothing but cuts, bruises, and idle speculation about what had happened to his old enemy; speculation that had gnawed at his soul until today. Thanks to this morning's briefing, he now knew McCabe had resurfaced and had allied himself with the Creed all over again, perhaps to redeem himself after he failed in Atlantis. Again, Hunter was left guessing in the dark, but whatever happened, both men knew they had a score to settle with one another.

He looked around the small plane's cabin. More than halfway into their transatlantic flight, the team had used the time in their own ways. While he had been trying to find out more information about Francisco de Gama and the compass stolen from Las Vegas, Amy had busied herself with the mission's strategic planning, which usually meant going over everything with a fine toothcomb right down to local weather and even the operational budget.

Blanco and Jodie had been playing cards and chatting quietly among themselves while Lewis was occupying his time researching everything he could about the *Titanic*. It was already a subject of great interest to the former Marine and he'd enjoyed getting stuck into it. At the back of the aircraft, a young Quinn Mosley was fast asleep, having hacked into Olav Skulberg's security camera archive and personal email accounts within the first hour of the flight.

They were, Hunter was starting to think, the very best team in the world in this field, and that made his occasional desire to return to UNESCO even harder to rationalise.

'Any ideas yet?' Amy asked, startling him.

'Sorry?'

She pointed at the pile of notes on his lap. Scrawled pencil ramblings, ideas, doodles. He'd drawn the ring and compass from memory, even though he had a picture of both of them in the briefing packs provided by Gates.

'Not really,' he said with a disarming grin. 'My specialist field is the ancient world. These artifacts are much later, coming from the sixteenth century, or thereabouts. But if McCabe is involved...' He paused. 'If the Creed is involved, then I'm sure the ancient world has something to do with it all, but until I know more I don't feel I can add too much value.'

'Don't be so hard on yourself,' she said.

Hunter felt his jaw tighten. 'If this is Creed, it's personal, Amy. We destroyed their chances of controlling the Atlantis site. They're going to want us dead in a big way. Kandarian was dangerous, but this is going to be much more dangerous. Everyone gets that, right?'

She nodded. 'Everyone gets it, and they're all still here.'

She looked into his eyes, seeing how much he cared for the other team members perhaps for the first time. The kidder had gone. She was looking at a serious army officer and experienced field archaeologist. A man on a mission determined to take care of those in his command.

Hunter looked back, a brief smile fading on his lips. He already knew, before they had touched down in Norway, that this mission was either going to make them or break them.

8

Olav Skulberg's mansion was every bit as impressive as Max Hunter had presumed it would be. His first sight of it was catching a vague glimpse of its hardwood and steel frame rising out of the Norwegian mist. As the small boat sailed closer to the private island, more details became clearer – two enormous glass windows on the property's façade, lit a dark orange by the interior lighting, were like giant eyes staring back at him. By the time they were mooring on the bleached jetty, even the electric razor-wire fence was visible.

The man piloting the luxury tender had introduced himself back in Sjølyst Marina as Arvid Olsen. Now, he skilfully navigated them through a maze of floating pontoons and brought them to a stop nearest the land. Hopping out of the vessel, he nimbly tied it to an aluminium mooring cleat and then invited the team to join him on dry land.

They stepped off the bobbing boat and onto the small island, then followed Olsen through a gate in the fence and along a smooth marble pathway leading up to the postmodern mansion. Exposed support beams from the angular roof were rising above them like some kind of ribcage, stripped bare of all flesh by hungry vultures.

'Nice place,' Quinn said from the back of the line.

Amy elbowed her in the ribs. 'Keep it down, Quinn. We're guests, not real estate agents.'

'Sorry.'

Olsen opened the front door and showed them inside a large, minimalist hallway. There was a strange atmosphere hanging in the air that reminded Amy of some kind of church or mausoleum. A solemnity that stopped the place feeling like someone's home and turned it into something else, something she couldn't quite describe. A solitary piece of furniture, a small Tasmanian blackwood table, hosted an antique vase full of delicate white flowers.

'They're pretty,' Amy said.

Olsen turned and smiled. 'Dendrophylax lindenii.'

'Sounds impressive.'

'I should hope so. These are Cuban ghost orchids, one of the rarest varieties in the world. Officially endangered as a species. Mr Skulberg is most concerned with preserving as much of the natural world as possible. He has devoted much of his life to funding projects around the world dedicated to fighting climate emergencies, particularly extinction emergencies. As you might imagine, he is mostly concerned with marine environmentalism. It's his second love after the *Titanic*.'

'Admirable,' Amy said.

'The admirable admiral,' whispered Hunter, earning him a disapproving look from her.

If Olsen heard the comment, he paid it no attention. 'Please wait here while I see if the admiral is ready to receive you.'

'Certainly,' Amy said, flashing a second glance at Hunter.

Moments later, Olsen returned. 'Admiral Skulberg will see you now.'

They followed him along a plain, white-painted corridor decorated with oil paintings of ships from across the ages and into a snug room at the back of the house. The assistant showed them inside, announced them, and then made himself scarce. Sitting beside a large roaring fireplace was a tall, broad-chested man with a fine shock of silver hair swept back from his forehead. He was holding a newspaper, but when he saw them, he folded it up and rose from his chair, reminding Hunter of the way an old and stately king might move.

'Hello and welcome to my home,' he said, taking care to shake everyone's hand. 'It's such a pleasure to see you here all safe, and I must say I am delighted finally to meet Jim's famous HARPA team. Please, take a seat around the fire while I pour some drinks. I hope single malt whisky is all right with everyone because that's all I keep in my little snug.'

A round of nodding heads gave him his answer.

'Excellent. It's a fine old drop, as you say in English.'

When Hunter saw the forty-year-old Glenfiddich, he was only too happy to accept a perfectly poured single measure in one of the admiral's heavy crystal tumblers. From what he understood about whisky, he knew he had well over one hundred and fifty dollars' worth in his hand, and the first long, slow sip did nothing to dissuade him of it.

'That's a beautiful drink, Admiral,' he said, raising his glass. '*Skål*.'

The old man's eyes sparkled but also narrowed when he heard the word. 'You speak Norwegian, Dr Hunter?'

'Not at all,' he said. 'I dated a woman from Bergen once, many years ago.'

Amy looked at him. 'You never told me that.'

He grinned. 'The personal life of Max Hunter is far too rich and complex to be given away just like that.' He snapped his fingers and smiled. 'Think of it like you would a medieval tapestry taking years to understand and appreciate.'

She shook her head. 'Sure, if you say so.'

'This woman from Bergen,' Jodie said. 'Why'd she dump ya, Hunter?'

'As a matter of fact,' he said, enjoying the conversation, 'it was a mutual decision to separate.'

'Yeah, sure.'

'Ah, young people!' Skulberg said. 'If only you knew how fast you get from your age to my age, you would waste much less time bickering. But now, we move on.' He resumed his seat, a deep, soft leather wingchair with a tweed blanket draped over the arm, and stretched his long legs out beside the fire. After a sip of whisky and a long, satisfied sigh, he said, 'First, thank you again for coming to see me at such short notice. I know how busy you are and I am grateful. I have followed your unclassified exploits with keen interest and I can only imagine the classified parts of your missions were even more fun.'

A long pause, then he laughed.

Amy looked awkward. 'Well...'

'Please, I'm not prying. I go back a long way with Jim Gates and as a former military man, I know why certain material and operations are classified. I have no interest in any of your secret government work. No, not at all. The reason I invited you here, as I know Jim will already have briefed you, is because I need your expertise. You are the best in your fields, after all, and you have such wonderful and extensive experience in retrieving valuable and rare relics stolen by smugglers and thieves. No one stands close to you.'

'That's kind of you to say so,' Amy said.

The reclusive multi-millionaire sipped more whisky, clearly relishing the company. 'Not at all, it's merely stating the truth. Here in this room, we have Dr Max Hunter, the world-famous archaeologist, formerly of UNESCO. Our very own Indiana Jones.'

Jodie almost spat her whisky into her glass but covered it up by pretending to cough. Amy flashed her a reprimanding glare as Skulberg continued his welcome speech.

'Agent Amy Fox of the FBI – one of the most accomplished professionals in this famous organisation and spoken of very highly by my old friend, Jim. We also have Sal Blanco, a veteran helicopter pilot from the US Army, Ben Lewis, a former US Marine, Jodie Priest, a woman who can break into anywhere on Earth without leaving a trace, and then, last but not least, the mysterious, enigmatic Quinn Mosley. The famous white hat hacker known throughout the technology underworld as Ghost.'

He twisted slightly in his chair until he was gazing at the young goth. She had drained her whisky and was staring right back at him without so much as a single blink.

'Hi.'

He laughed. 'A young lady with computer skills superior to the next ten best hackers combined. I presume you have already been inside my computer system and had a good poke around on your way over on the plane, no?'

Quinn looked anxiously at Amy.

'Fear not, Agent Mosley,' Skulberg continued. 'I would expect nothing less from you, or the rest of this team. This is why you are the best. Besides, I know what you found in my computer system and email trails and that is precisely nothing of interest because I have nothing to hide.'

'Of course not, sir,' Amy said.

'And if I did want to hide anything, then it would be written in ink on paper and locked in a secret safe somewhere. In this day and age, this is more than ever the safest way to guard a confidence, wouldn't you say?'

'Moscow certainly does,' she said. 'The Kremlin ordered the use of typewriters again for the most confidential documents nearly ten years ago. There's no hacking those things.'

The old admiral grinned and took a long sip of whisky, finishing off his glass.

'No, there is no hacking those things, especially if the documents they produce are locked away in safes.' His smile slowly faded and he began to look tired. The fire crackling in the hearth flickered on his face and lit up the deep lines and wrinkles on it, making him look much older than before.

'Safes can be cracked,' Jodie said. 'Take my word for it.'

'Yes, very true,' Skulberg said. 'But as I say, I have nothing to hide at all, but I agree with what you say about safes. The most secret things of all I keep not even in safes, but in the only place I trust and nowhere else. Do you know where that is, young people?'

Amy shook her head.

'In my head, Agent Fox.' He tapped his temple. 'Right in here, where not even Agent Mosley and her terrifying computer skills, or Agent Priest and her incredible safe-cracking skills, can find it.'

'Sounds like a challenge,' Quinn said.

Jodie crossed her legs and sipped her whisky. 'Sure does.'

Skulberg laughed and slapped his knee. Amy guessed the old recluse was enjoying the company more than he might let on. Maybe his guard was slipping. She recalled when Gates told them how he believed his old Norwegian friend was keeping something back from him and sensed an opportunity to pounce. 'Admiral, I think despite your protestations, you might be hiding something from us, or at the very least not giving us the whole story.'

His grin broke into a broad smile. He could hide it no longer. 'Yes, I think I might be, but it's probably not what you think. I'm taking it that you've all heard of the robbery at the Luxor Las Vegas by now?'

Amy exchanged a short glance with her team and ended up looking at

Hunter. The English soldier simply shrugged his shoulders. 'Yes, we heard about that,' Amy said. 'You have something to say about it?'

'Of course,' he said. 'Something that might surprise you very much. But first, I see from your glasses that everyone needs another drink. Let me help you all with that.'

As Admiral Skulberg rose from his chair, moaning about his creaking bones, Amy and Hunter caught each other's glance one more time. She looked at the rest of her team while Skulberg poured the drinks; it looked like they were all as intrigued as she was. When he'd handed the tumblers back to their owners, Skulberg sank down into his chair by the fire, stared at them with serious, sombre eyes, and started talking.

'This is a story that goes back a long way,' he said quietly. 'A family story, and I'll only say it once, so pay attention. It might just save your lives.'

9

'It begins in the early part of the last century, and it starts not here in Norway but London. My grandfather was a brilliant man named Harald Skulberg and he was the Norwegian ambassador to the United Kingdom for fifteen years, from 1899 to 1914. He returned to Oslo in the summer of 1914 when the Great War broke out. Norway was a neutral state in that conflict, but he wanted to return in case that changed.'

He sipped his whisky, leaned forward, and jabbed at the logs in the grate with a long black poker. Then when he was satisfied with the fire's progress, he returned to the comforts of his chair and continued the story of Harald Skulberg.

'My grandfather was not merely a diplomat, but also an avid collector of exotic and rare relics from the ancient world. This collection he took with him to London when his tenure at the embassy began in the spring of 1899. This collection was not vast, but it was respectable and included many valuable objects. Two of his most prized possessions were a gold and emerald ring and a small golden statue.'

Hunter fought the smile away from his lips. 'I think we might be getting somewhere.'

Skulberg's smile was broader. 'I thought you'd like this bit, Dr Hunter. But please, allow me to continue. The ring was a typical Spanish fleet treasure ring, cast of pure gold and the highest quality emerald, most likely mined in Colombia.' Here, he paused and a frown darkened his lined face as he reached over to the shelf beside his chair and picked up a black and white photograph. 'The statue was a strange thing – here is a picture of it, Dr Hunter. As you can see, the image is very old, taken by my grandfather in the early 1900s. His signature and the date are written on the back in his own handwriting.'

Hunter took the faded and torn picture and carefully examined the image of the statue. Six inches high, smooth gold body and face but with a more detailed headdress, the figure was some kind of mountain god. 'Muisca, not Incan. AD 1300 to 1400, I'd say, but probably closer to the former. Judging from some of the detail on the headdress, I would also venture a guess it's from the central Colombian highlands.'

Skulberg's frown turned back into a warm smile. 'Already you have given me something I did not know. The last expert who saw that picture told me it was much older.'

'I don't think so,' Hunter said confidently. 'The goldsmithing is too fine, especially around the headdress, as I say. It's most likely Sué, the ancient sun god, but the picture is so old and many of these gods are somewhat similar in appearance when rendered in gold like this, I can't be completely certain.'

Skulberg nodded, satisfied. 'I don't think that's important at this time, Dr Hunter. But what is important is that back in 1912, when my grandfather was still working in London, thieves broke into his home and stole just two items – the ring and the statue. What bothered him so much was that he had so many more valuable items in the collection and yet the thieves overlooked them all and went out of their way to steal only the ring and the statue.'

'So they had some kind of value above the base gold and emeralds?' Amy asked.

'Yes, without a doubt.'

Blanco scratched his jaw, as he often did when he was thinking. 'What happened after they were stolen?'

'The robbery was planned intricately and executed the day before a ship set sail for the United States. This was to enable the thieves to steal the objects, travel down to Southampton to board the ship, and make their escape with the stolen goods. The name of that ship was the *Titanic*.'

He stopped talking. The only sound in the room was the crackling of the fire in the grate.

'What happened to the thieves?' Lewis asked.

Skulberg shrugged. 'Grandfather never even knew their names, but he knew they had stolen the objects to order. You see, the Skulberg family has a rival, another family – a very powerful family from Austria called the Bauers. This family has competed with us for artifacts for nearly two hundred years. The head of the family back then was an amateur archaeologist of dubious repute called Ernst Bauer who once offered my grandfather a ludicrous sum of money for the ring and the statue. My grandfather refused, naturally. They were rivals.'

'What happened after he refused?' asked Jodie.

'A few weeks later, these thieves broke into his London home and stole the two very same objects desired by Bauer. Both my grandfather and my father and me are all very clear on the matter. Ernst Bauer ordered the robbery. And the plot gets thicker.'

He leaned over to his bookshelf once again and pulled a piece of paper off the top of the books. Crumpled and yellowed, it looked like it had been folded and refolded a million times. This time, he handed it to Amy.

'What's this?' she asked. 'A list of names?'

'A list of passengers who sailed on the *Titanic*,' Skulberg said respectfully. 'If you look at the top you will see a section of three hundred and twenty-four names. These are the names of the passengers who travelled in first class.'

She was already running her finger down the list. Not too far down from the top she stopped and gasped. 'Professor Ernst Bauer!'

Skulberg frowned. 'Ernst Bauer was no professor. He was an amateur and he operated entirely without ethics. Some say he was merely a puppet for a much more sinister organisation, but my family has never been able to prove this, and neither do we think it matters. All that matters is that he ordered the thieves to steal the ring and statue and to hand them over to him on board the *Titanic*. This way, he could make good his escape with the stolen goods.'

'They went down with the ship?' Ben's tone was sombre.

'Bauer certainly did. He was never on the list of survivors. As for the thieves – possibly, but there's no way to tell. We never knew their names.'

'How did you find the ring and compass?' Jodie said. 'At some kind of auction?'

Skulberg's face broke into a smile. 'No, no auction, Agent Priest. You see, in 1984, I funded an expedition, a salvage mission, if you will, to the *Titanic*.'

Hunter, like the rest of the group, was visibly surprised and impressed. 'Wait, you dived down to the wreck?'

'I certainly did,' Skulberg said. 'Back in 1984. It was in all the newspapers. My fifteen minutes of fame. I wasn't the first, but we broke some records for the length of time down there and the amount of the wreck we surveyed before coming back to the surface. Good times.'

'Was it a success?' asked Amy.

'Partly. Using the extensive details of first-class passengers, we were able to locate Ernst Bauer's room. His criminal accumulation of money through relic hunting and smuggling was not able to provide him with a parlour suite – over $120,000 in today's money – but he was able to buy himself a single-person berth in first class, as you saw from the list. Luckily, his berth was in a part of the ship with the hull ripped away so we were able to access it with our submersible. Using the robotic arm, I was able to find and recover my grandfather's ring in an upturned jewellery box on the floor.'

'Whoa,' said Quinn. 'That is actually pretty amazing.'

'Welcome back to the conversation, Agent Mosley,' Skulberg said with a warm smile.

Quinn huffed out a sigh and pulled her hoodie back up over her head. 'Whatever.'

Skulberg took no offence. He turned back to Amy and the others and continued with the story he was telling them. 'It was the greatest day of my life.'

'But you didn't find your grandfather's statue?' Blanco asked.

Skulberg sighed and shook his head. 'You see, when the *Titanic* sank, she broke into two pieces.'

'Yeah, I saw the movie,' Jodie said.

'It wasn't quite as dramatic as either of the movies,' said Lewis.

'Agent Lewis is right,' said Skulberg, resuming control of his tale. 'The ship broke in two as the second movie portrays, but at a much shallower angle. When the front section of the ship went down, its bow went first and she went down hard and fast, cutting through the water like a knife, just as she was designed to do. It hit the ocean floor, nearly four kilometres deep at that location, very hard, and crumpled onto the seabed, ejecting pieces of the ship for hundreds of metres all over the place.'

'Four kilometres?' Jodie asked. 'What's that to a high-school dropout from California?'

'Nearly two and a half miles,' Hunter said. 'Or twelve and a half thousand feet.'

'Almost half the height of Mount Everest,' Amy said.

'Deep, then,' said a muffled voice behind Quinn's hoodie.

'Yes, deep,' Skulberg said, growing more serious. 'And when you're down there, it's a totally different world. Pitch black, silent. Frightening, actually. People have seen the pictures of the *Titanic* on the seabed and that is how they visualise it, but naturally, unless there is a sub down there with a light, it's in total darkness all the time. Barely any sunlight gets deeper than two hundred metres, never mind four thousand metres. You cannot imagine the blackness down there if you switch the lights off.'

After a long pause, Amy broke the silence. 'You were telling us about when the *Titanic* crashed onto the ocean floor.'

'Indeed, I was. The impact of the crash was considerable and it caused a great deal of damage to much of the ship's interior. Many of the berths and cabins were crushed beyond recognition. I was lucky that I was able to get into Bauer's berth with the sub because, as I say, the outside wall was completely ripped off at that point on the hull, but this was a double-edge sword because much of his possessions must have been ejected and sprayed out over the seabed. After finding the ring he stole from my grandfather, I searched in adjoining cabins and all over the debris field, but I could not find the statue. Eventually, we had to resurface.'

'You didn't go back down?' Lewis asked.

'No. It's a very expensive and dangerous thing to do, and we knew the chances of finding it after our previous search were low. We sailed back to Boston and that was the end of the mission. It was a truly remarkable and memorable time in my life for which I am very grateful, but the failure to find the idol has been an incessant itch that can never be scratched. I'm sure you have similar experiences in your endeavour to locate other archaeological relics, Dr Hunter?'

Hunter nodded. 'A list as long as your arm.'

'What about going back again?' Lewis asked, clearly enthralled by the story.

Skulberg shook his head. 'Relic hunters have caused an enormous amount of damage picking over the ship's carcass for so many years that today it's much harder to get permission to dive there.'

'It certainly is,' Hunter said. 'In fact, in 2012, exactly one century after the tragedy, it was made a UNESCO site and is protected by that status just like any other UNESCO site. It used to be that anyone with the capital to fund a dive could just sail right out there and search the wreck for goodies, but not any more, and rightly so, in my view.'

'Perhaps you are right, Dr Hunter,' said Skulberg.

The fire crackled and popped.

'At least you got the ring,' Amy said, trying to comfort him.

The old devil grinned. 'And one other thing.'

Skulberg reached down beside his chair and the wall and pulled another photograph into view. 'Dr Hunter may be right about restricting access to the wreck, but then, if it weren't for my dive, we would not also have this.'

10

Skulberg showed them a picture of the compass they had seen back in Gates's briefing.

'Francisco de Gama's compass,' Amy said.

The admiral nodded. 'Yes, it surely is.'

'And recently stolen in Vegas,' said Blanco.

Skulberg nodded. 'The very same. You see, when I was down at the wreck searching for the ring and statue, I happened to find this compass in Bauer's berth.'

'Back in 1912, the ring and statue were stolen from your grandfather,' Amy said. 'But not the compass. Shouldn't that go to Ernst Bauer's family?'

Skulberg laughed. 'Not at all. Marine salvage is like war... To the victor go the spoils. In this case, I kept the ring and Morton kept the compass.'

'Morton Woolf?' Hunter asked, already knowing the answer.

'Yes, Morton co-funded the salvage operation with me back in 1984.' His voice trailed away as he looked at the image of the compass, then the image of the ring. 'Luckily gold does not tarnish, but we needed to do some restoration work on the gem and a few other areas. Now, it's as beautiful as the day it was made. Morton chose to leave the compass in its original condition. That's his style.'

'They're both incredible artifacts,' said Jodie.

'Thank you, Agent Priest,' Skulberg said with a smile.

'Jim believes these robberies are linked,' Amy said. 'Can you help us with that?'

He paused, lifting his tired eyes from the pictures and watching a thick dull blanket of mist drift past his window, then he returned his gaze to the warm, flickering fire. 'Yes, I can help you with this. The ring that was stolen from this very museum a few days ago, the compass that was stolen in Las Vegas, and the statue that remains lost to the depths, were all once owned by Francisco de Gama.'

Amy and Hunter exchanged a cautious glance.

'You had to see that coming,' said Quinn's muffled voice.

'This is no secret,' said Skulberg. 'These artifacts are all very special. Long before the ring belonged to my grandfather and long before the compass belonged to Ernst Bauer, they were in the possession of Francisco de Gama, the Spanish explorer. He also once owned the missing golden statue.'

Before anyone could speak, Skulberg went on.

'And being aware of this and the theft of de Gama's compass from the exhibition in Las Vegas, perhaps now you see why I was concerned enough to contact Jim Gates. You can see now how these robberies are linked. The thieves have specifically targeted my museum and the exhibition in Las Vegas to steal these objects at the same time. Something about these relics has driven these men to hunt them down and steal them. I want to know why.'

'We think we know the identity of one of the thieves,' Amy said. 'His name is—'

'Brodie McCabe.' Skulberg's voice was ice.

Hunter's head turned. 'You know McCabe?'

'Not personally, no, but I know he was part of the raid. He did not, however, orchestrate either of the robberies. I believe this was done by a man named Hans Bauer, a high-ranking member of the group you call the Creed.'

Amy said, 'You mean...'

Before she finished, Skulberg grimaced. 'Yes, Ernst Bauer's grandson. I believe he is the man behind these robberies. He ordered McCabe to do it.'

Another long silence.

'The feud goes on another generation, then,' said Blanco.

Before the Norwegian could reply, Amy said, 'Why not tell this to Jim?'

'First, I don't trust that the phone lines aren't being tapped. If you know how the Creed operates you know how Bauer operates. Tapping phones is a piece of cake for people like this. Second, I might know Jim but I had never even seen any of you. I can't trust a man or woman until I have looked them in the eye and shared a glass of whisky with them. I made up my mind that I trusted all of you before any of you had finished your first glass.'

'Ain't that grand,' Quinn said. 'We just passed a job interview.'

'Yes, you did,' Skulberg said flatly. 'Your skills as relic retrieval specialists are becoming renowned in all the right circles, and some of the wrong ones too. Now, I want to hire you to retrieve my stolen ring, and the stolen compass if you can get it, from Bauer and bring them to me.'

'But the compass belongs to Morton Woolf.'

'Not any more,' Skulberg said. 'I bought it from him a few hours ago for a considerable sum.'

'Even though it might never be recovered?' Hunter asked.

'I have total faith in you,' Skulberg said. 'So, stop drinking my whisky and go get my artifacts back.'

'But where do we start?' Amy said. 'Did they leave any clues in your museum?'

'No, they were professional in that regard.'

'I still don't get where we start then,' said Jodie.

'You start with more faith,' Skulberg said. 'I know in my heart Hans Bauer is behind these robberies. I might not know why exactly, but I know it was him. You start by visiting him at his home in Austria.'

'Could you be more precise?' Amy asked. 'Austria is a big place.'

'And so is his home.' Skulberg got up from his chair and pulled a final picture from the open book on his shelf. It featured the biggest castle any of them had ever seen before, perched in dark black mountains and surrounded by tall fir trees. Above, a low, leaden sky promised cold, heavy rain. 'This is the Schloss Kapfenstein high in the Austrian Alps. Herr Bauer inherited it from his father and so on back to the Middle Ages. Some say this dreadful place is where Bauer's weird Creed cult meets at certain times of the year to discuss their business. I neither know about this nor care about this. I care only about my business and what belongs to me. The idol might be lost to history, but my heart tells me the ring and the compass are here.'

Amy was still and silent, wondering just what the hell Gates had gotten them into. Spanish explorers, rings, compasses, golden statues. The *Titanic*. Cults and castles. McCabe and the Creed. Then, she remembered what she was paid to do, and why HARPA had been established in the first place.

'We'll do our best to retrieve the items stolen from you, Admiral,' she said.

* * *

Olav Skulberg watched the HARPA team follow Arvid Olsen back down the path and climb into the small tender. As they turned in the water and slowly faded away in the sea fog, he set down his whisky tumbler and lit a cigar. Then, he used an intercom to summon another man into the snug. The man entered moments later. He was tall and well-built with a gymnast's physique, short black hair, and a clipped, neat beard. He wore a black shirt and black trousers and walked with the casual but confident grace of a duke.

'You called, sir?'

Skulberg stared into the fog and blew out a thick cloud of cigar smoke. 'They've gone.'

Jørgen Dahl nodded once. 'I know. How did it go, sir?'

'Well, I think. Gates was right about them. They're more than up to the job. Perhaps a little too up to it.'

'Will that be a problem?'

Skulberg took a seat, set the cigar down in an ashtray, and formed his hands into a scholar's cradle as he stared into the fire once again. Deep in thought, he shook his head. 'I don't think so. I want a comprehensive progress report on Njord as soon as possible.'

Njord. The word hit the air like a hammer striking an anvil.

'I can prepare a written report within the hour,' said Dahl.

'No, I think it's better if I speak with the man himself.'

'I'll make some calls and see if he's available, sir. Would you like some coffee in the meantime?'

'No, and that will be all, Jørgen. No more interruptions until you've set up the call.'

'Of course, Admiral.'

'And make sure that this business continues to stay only between us and him. No one must know the truth about what we're doing. Not even them,' he said, gesturing out into the misty water beyond the window. 'Not even Gates. It's too important. Too dangerous. Nothing can jeopardise Njord. Nothing. I won't allow it.'

'Yes, sir.'

Skulberg heard Dahl click the heavy oak door shut and then he rearranged the mostly burnt-out logs on the fire. He relit his cigar on the glowing embers and sank into his faithful, old armchair. He took a long, deep draw and savoured the rich taste of the smoke. His blood had come up a little when he'd talked about Njord to his loyal private assistant, Dahl. He could feel it in his cheeks.

But now, the peaceful crackling of the fire in the grate and its gentle, reassuring warmth was lulling him into one of his daydreams. Not dreams of wealth; he had more money than he could possibly spend. These were dreams of another kind. Dreams of power and glory. With the cigar slowly burning out in his fingers, he slipped away into sleep as the fire beside him gradually turned to ash.

11

When the HARPA jet neared the end of its approach, Innsbruck ATC tower vectored it to descend through a valley to the east. This involved a sharp bank to starboard before lining up ready for 'short final'. Hunter watched the snow-capped mountains flash past the aircraft as they landed, and was reminded of the day he flew into Switzerland with Klara Steiner. She had turned out to be a traitor working for the Creed, but the Swiss billionaire she worked for, Oskar Rorschach, had become a good friend to the team and even lent them his submarine yacht, the *Seawolf*, to help them win the race to Atlantis.

'Wish I had time for some skiing,' he muttered to himself, looking longingly at the slopes.

'I'd pay to see that,' said Jodie as the plane touched down and roared down to taxi speed.

'And I would happily take your money,' he said with a wink.

They zoomed through Austrian customs and walked outside into a light snowfall. Gates had already organised transport with Europcar and after a few minutes shuffling through some paperwork with the small office, a young woman wrapped in a thick fur coat showed them outside and told them where to find their hired SUV. They piled their gear into the back and Blanco took the wheel. Seconds later, he was driving over the Sieglangersteg bridge and pulling right onto the eastbound carriage of the Inntal Autobahn.

With night falling, dusk gathered over the mountain peaks and the clouds darkened. Hunter was sitting in the back beside Quinn, earbuds in and eyes closed. There was some kind of mix on his iPod created by Quinn, involving something she had called 'future garage'. He had no idea what it meant, but it was okay, so he kept listening. He watched the cars race past on the other side of the autobahn. Expensive and new, mostly. On the other side of the car, the town's streetlights sparkled on the surface of the black and gloomy River Inn.

As the built-up area slipped behind them and they went deeper into the valleys, mountains pocked with ancient churches stretched up high above them and disappeared into the dank clouds scratching the night. He yawned, tipped his head back, and watched the snowflakes rip past the sunroof. As always, the mission was unfolding all around him at the speed of light. Soon, they would be at the castle, but he hoped a confrontation with Hans Bauer was still avoidable.

The plan to infiltrate Schloss Kapfenstein had been planned by the team on the plane as soon as it left Oslo Gardermoen Airport back in Norway. Before they had reached full cruising altitude, Quinn had already broken into the castle's security system and taken a full inventory of everything it had to offer. It was then she found time to make the mix for his iPod, delivering it with a message in sombre tones: 'Listen to this and pay attention, Grandpa.' He had smiled and accepted the gift in good grace. This was Ghost's way.

After a long, tiring drive, the team was finally reaching their destination high in the Tyrolean Alps to the south of Innsbruck. When Hunter saw the outline of Bauer's castle against the sky, he was instantly reminded of another castle he had visited with the HARPA team – Schloss Schwarzenfels, or Black Rock Castle. That hideous place was located in Germany's Bavarian mountains, not a million miles from here, and had served as one of the Creed's main headquarters. Owned by an international consortium of shareholders, it had been impossible to use its discovery to track down the Creed's elite but long after they had left the place, Gates had reported something far more sinister to the team than anything Hunter could have imagined.

Deep in Black Rock Castle's dungeon, the authorities had uncovered evidence of some kind of terrible beast in a deep dugout pit. Snapped, splintered, and broken human bones had been found littering its floor. They had also found long, deep gouges carved into the pit's walls by some unknown creature. All they knew about those terrible tooth and claw marks was that whatever had made them must have been significantly larger than any mammal known to man.

And even presuming it was a mammal was mere speculation; whatever it was had been taken away by the Creed long before anyone else could find it.

Hunter repressed a shudder and tried to put the thought behind him, but it was impossible. If McCabe and the Creed really were involved in this mission, if Bauer was Creed, then... just maybe, whatever the hell the Creed had moved out of that pit in Bavaria was now here, in Schloss Kapfenstein. That was a thought that did not bear thinking about, right alongside why the Creed would want a creature like that in their possession in the first place. Was it for ritual purposes? For punishments? Was it kept to terrorise their members and keep them in line? Hunter tried even harder to get the thought of it out of his mind.

He was helped along by the sound of Amy's voice, soft but determined in the darkness of the SUV. 'Just a little further, Sal. We can park up here on the left in some kind of lane.'

Blanco found the place she meant and brought the SUV to a stop. When he killed the engine, the sound of the howling wind and driving snow filled the car. As they unbuckled seats and organised weapons, Quinn was already preparing a mini-briefing about the vast property's security.

'Listen up. Nothing has changed since I hacked into their system back on the plane but there are more guards now – or at least more guards with cell phones. Any Luddites without cell phones, I cannot track.'

'That makes them smart, not Luddites,' Hunter said.

'They'll all have phones,' Amy said. 'They're security and being in contact at all times will be part of their contracts.'

'Right,' Quinn said. 'That's what I was thinking. Using my own proprietary product designed to detect Wi-Fi and Bluetooth signals in real-time, I have determined that right now there are seven of them on shift at the castle. Six with smartphones and one with a much older one, probably a burner. Nokia, I think.'

'Wait,' Hunter said. 'How can you detect an old Nokia that's not even on Wi-Fi?'

'I can still detect them from their cellular signals alone, which means not even burners or older non-smartphones can hide from my web of evil.'

'That's great work, Quinn,' Blanco said.

'Sure is,' said Amy.

Quinn brushed off the compliments. 'So, obviously for the smartphone, I hacked into their accounts' location services to be able to track them wherever they go. This works unless they disable their location services, but they're probably not going to work that out until it's too late. Even if that happens, we have the cellular signal detection facility.'

'Yeah, really good work, Quinn,' said Amy as she pulled her beanie down on her head. 'How are we identifying them individually?'

'There are seven of them, so… it's obvious, right?'

'Not to me it isn't,' Hunter said.

Quinn sighed. 'Doc, Grumpy, Happy, Sleepy… Snow White and the Seven Dwarfs, okay?'

Lewis laughed. 'I love it. Who could forget that?'

'Exactly,' Quinn said. 'I'll monitor their locations in real-time right here from the comfort of the SUV while you guys go inside the castle and locate the ring and compass. Easy, right?'

Amy checked her gun and slid it into her holster. 'Easy is not the word I was going to use, Quinn. Everyone, let's go. And keep this as quiet and professional as possible. Better we can locate the goods without causing a disturbance, but if not, then so be it. We don't know the full importance of these artifacts yet, but we do know Skulberg is still probably keeping something from us, and we're going to need to know what that is.'

'And there's only one way, right?' Jodie said.

'Right,' Amy said. 'And it's inside Castle Grayskull. Let's move.'

12

Hunter was first, leading the small team from the front as he made his way through the forest at the base of the castle's eastern aspect. The snow had stopped falling now but the night was dark and moonless and this was unlikely to change; the clouds were low and thick and skidded over the castle's turrets, driven by a powerful and icy easterly wind.

Each member of the team was wearing all-black combat fatigues and they had their faces covered in black camo grease. They each wore a small, compact backpack and everyone was ready for what had been planned as a lightning raid on Bauer's mountain hideout. As they approached the castle's northern wall, they slowed down and crept at a walking pace, careful not to give their position away by making any unnecessary noise.

'We're in position,' Hunter said into his comms.

They heard Quinn's quiet voice back in the safety of the SUV. 'Copy that. I have your GPS locations on the grid. Right now, you're on your own, but Doc and Grumpy are both moving in your direction. From the castle's blueprints, I'd say they're either on a section of the roof or in a corridor inside but there's no way for me to get elevation data from their location services. Or from anywhere else, before anyone asks.'

'Got it,' he said. 'How long till they're at our position?'

'Two minutes.'

'Thanks.'

He turned in the darkness, barely able to make out the faces of his friends in the black of night. 'Everyone heard what she just said. We have two minutes to get up over this wall and into the inner perimeter. Is everyone ready?'

'We're all good, right?' Amy said.

Blanco and Jodie nodded. Lewis gave a thumbs up.

Hunter made his way over to the outer wall and used the grappling hook inside his pack, swinging it to gain momentum and then releasing it. It flew through the air and landed on top of the wall, its steel hooks firmly gripping the sides of one of the crenelations. He started to scale it, getting almost to the top before the clouds broke to reveal a bright full moon, climbing high in the sky above the castle. This he had not expected, but the high wind had broken a gap in the clouds, bathing him in a silvery light. He tucked his head down, stopped moving, and waited for the clouds to swallow it back up again.

Thrown back into darkness, he restarted the climb, reaching the top in a few seconds. After improving the hook's purchase in the stone crenelation and checking the coast was clear, he radioed down for the rest of the team to join him. Jodie was next, then Lewis, then Amy, and then Blanco. All five of them crouched low as they made their way along the top of the wide, medieval wall. They were heading to a turret maybe twenty yards ahead of them. To their right, mountain slopes were carpeted in pine trees and snow. To their left were the main grounds of the castle – a vast courtyard and smaller buildings scattered around a grand and imposing Austrian Schloss.

'We're almost there,' Amy said. 'Keep going.'

'Wait!' Hunter hushed them and waved them to a stop. In front of the team by just a few short metres, he saw a man's silhouette on the other side of the turret. Dropping his voice to a whisper, he spoke into the comms. 'Wait. Looks like Grumpy's come back for another look.'

He froze in the turret's shadow, tucked up tight against the cold stone wall, and waited for Grumpy to pass. He could have reached out and grabbed him, maybe got him in a chokehold and thrown him over the wall, but it was too risky. He had lost Doc's location and was unable to communicate with Quinn because Grumpy was just too close.

Then, it all kicked off. The man they had designated Grumpy turned around to head back to the turret. He caught a glimpse of Hunter in the shadows and reached for his gun. From where his hand was going, Hunter guessed it must be a handgun in a shoulder holster, but luckily his large winter coat was so substantial it slowed him down for long enough for Hunter to act.

He leaped out of the shadows and struck the man in the face with a bone-crunching punch, snapping his head back and triggering a loud and angry grunt. Hunter wasn't done and as soon as the man squared back up to him, he headbutted him hard in the face, splitting his lips open and breaking his nose.

Jodie winced.

Amy gasped, clapping her hand over her mouth. 'Max!'

Doc arrived out of nowhere, leaping through the turret door and coming to the aid of his battered associate. He scanned the team and headed straight for Lewis, reaching for a weapon as he pounded over to him through the ice and snow.

'Give me your best,' Lewis said.

The man struck him hard, a solid blow to his temple that almost knocked Lewis off his feet. The blow broke open the skin above his left eye and blood ran down over his face. Even with the pain radiating into his head, the young ex-Marine wasn't fazed by the strike. Instead, he lunged forward and went on the offensive, leaping sideways at the last minute to avoid the man's second attack and then powering his own fist up into his opponent's jaw, breaking it in two and sending him skidding over on the ice and cracking the back of his head on the flagstones below.

'Doc's over and out,' Lewis called out. 'Bastard took me at my word and really did give his best.' He was rubbing his temple and sweeping some blood out of his eye. The first thing he saw was Jodie and Amy standing behind Blanco just as Grumpy got the better of Hunter and drove a hard jab into his chin.

He moved in for the kill, but Blanco now dashed forward and grabbed Grumpy's shoulders, stopping him from landing another blow on Hunter. He spun him around and punched him in his face, already nicely softened up by the Englishman. The snow swirled and the wind howled. On Doc's belt, his radio crackled. Someone was speaking in very fast and anxious German.

'Looks like we might get rumbled soon,' Jodie said, switching the radio off.

'Then let's get moving,' said Amy. 'We have to get over to the main building and start our search there. I doubt Bauer would leave his precious artifacts out of his sight.'

'What's happening?' Quinn asked.

Hunter briefed her. 'Grumpy turned out to be a hardened former Austrian commando at well over six and a half feet tall.'

'But he really does look grumpy though,' Jodie said with a shrug. 'Gotta give that to you, Quinn.'

They went inside the turret and descended a stone spiral staircase until they reached the courtyard at the bottom. Across the yard, a large double doorway promised entry into the main section of Bauer's Schloss. It was situated behind a low stone wall, decorated with statues and gargoyles, another arched doorway in the centre of it – the final obstacle.

'Let's move,' Hunter said.

They ran across the courtyard and Amy vaulted over the metal rail and landed with a thud, gun in hand. Hunter was off to her left and slightly behind her. Lewis and Jodie were behind him and Blanco at the rear. Together, Hunter and Amy reached the door and slammed up against the wall on either side of it.

'Ready?' she said.

'On three,' Hunter said. 'One, two... three!'

He kicked the door open and they charged inside, guns raised into the aim.

'We're clear!' Amy called out into the comms.

'Nope,' Quinn said in their earpieces. 'You're not clear. You have three guys – Bashful, Sneezy, and Dopey – on their way over to you right now.'

'Where?' Hunter asked.

'They're right on top of you!' she said.

Jodie spun around and scanned for any sign of the enemy. 'I don't see them!'

'Then they're either above or below you,' said Quinn.

'Above,' Amy said. 'I hear their footsteps – listen!'

Before anyone could react, a klaxon sounded and the entire courtyard was lit up by a dozen piercingly bright arc lights.

'Did any of us order those lights to go on just to make this easier?' Hunter said.

'No,' Amy said, frowning. 'And this is no time for humour.'

'No, I guess not. And this is not a good development.'

Five men with compact machine pistols burst out of the castle entrance.

'Drop your weapons and raise your hands!' said one with a black and silver beard and a scar running down his cheek.

'That one is not Cheerful,' Hunter whispered. 'I don't care what Quinn says.'

'Silence!' another shouted.

A third man stepped forward. 'You will come with us. Mr Bauer has been expecting you.'

13

The men ordered them inside the castle and up a broad, stone staircase off to the right. It was dark, lit only with flickering beeswax pillar candles set inside ornate alcoves all over the stone walls. The men stayed well back, MP5s and MP7s gripped firmly and held up into the aim, muzzles pointing at the team's backs. Any funny business, Amy knew, and they would be riddled with lead in a heartbeat. Skulberg's cosy little snug back in Oslo now seemed very far away and her apartment in Washington may as well have been on another planet.

'Keep going!' one of the men barked. 'And turn left at the top of the steps.'

They were into an enormous baroque space, lit with more candles and covered in dark wood panelling. From some hidden speakers, a sombre string quartet played eerie music. Heavy, purple velvet drapes hung down at the sides of lead-lined windows and one of the walls was a giant bookcase, filled with thousands of leather-bound tomes. In the centre of the room, in front of a strange dais, was a large Persian rug, an intricate red and cream weave of two hideous beasts fighting over a giant pomegranate.

'Ah, welcome to my home.'

Amy shivered when she heard the voice. It came from a dark corner over to her right. When a man stepped out into the candlelight, she knew it could only be Hans Bauer.

'Some home,' Blanco said.

'And it's not a welcome if you have a gun trained on someone,' Hunter said.

Bauer walked over to them, his heels clicking on the wooden floorboards. Their sharp sound was muted when he reached the rug. 'Yes, how rude of me. Zeller! Send the men back to their quarters, but you remain outside this room, just in case our guests decide to betray my beneficent hospitality.'

'Sir.'

Zeller and the others quietly left the room.

'I won't ask why you have broken into my home this evening,' Bauer said. 'I already know this. I know everything about you. Your names, who you work for, your home addresses, your families' names and addresses. You are here tonight to try to steal two items I recently expended much time and effort returning to their rightful place, Schloss Kapfenstein.'

Amy said, 'You mean the ring you stole from Admiral Skulberg and the compass you stole from Morton Woolf.'

Bauer's thin face turned to her, icy eyes and sunken cheeks. 'The ring and the compass were both in the possession of my family in the nineteenth century. They were stolen by Eirik Skulberg, Admiral Skulberg's great grandfather. Yes, you may well exchange an uncertain glance with one another. Is he telling the truth, you ask? Can Bauer be trusted? Is this just more lies to cloud our judgement? No, they are not lies. He stole it and then the Skulberg family possessed those artifacts for nearly one hundred years before my own grandfather, Ernst Bauer, liberated them from the admiral's grandfather in 1912. No doubt Olav has bored you with the story already.'

'We have no reason to believe you,' Amy said, 'and even if what you say is true, there are legal channels to pursue. Whether or not they once belonged to your family is for the law to decide, not for you just to steal them.'

Bauer laughed. 'I can see you're a well-trained law enforcement officer. But there is no time to waste hiring an army of lawyers and filing endless legal documents. I must have the Bauer family artifacts back at once. There is no time to waste. The five ancient de Gama relics must be brought together if the prophecy is to be fulfilled.'

'I don't understand,' Hunter said. 'What do you mean "five"?'

Another chuckle. 'What do you call a group of people blundering around in the dark without a clue?'

They stared back at him in silence.

'Team HARPA!' He chuckled some more. 'You really have no idea what any of this is about, do you? Skulberg pulls Gates's strings and then he sends you out here, into the heart of the Creed without a single, pathetic clue.'

Amy flicked a glance at Hunter. The others stared at each other, their worst fears confirmed.

'Yes, that's right. What you have heard is true. The Bauer family is an ancient Creed bloodline. Now, we are charged with the acquisition of the five sacred relics. We will fulfil this duty with pride and efficiency.'

'What five relics?' Hunter asked.

Bauer looked at him like he was insane. 'The ring, the compass, the chalice, the crucifix, and the idol, Dr Hunter. De Gama's five sacred relics. Francisco de Gama, a man hunted for his membership in a very evil association with extremely dangerous beliefs. This is why he hid the relics, to ensure the Inquisition, who of course considered de Gama's association message to be blasphemous, would never find them. And this is why he fled, of course. But to where one can only speculate. I have my theories.'

'What was the significance of his five relics?' Hunter asked. 'Why are people dying in their pursuit?'

Bauer smiled and slipped a hand into his pocket as he began to strut up and down the vast room, enjoying every last ounce of the advantage he had over the famous team. 'On each one, de Gama inscribed a special clue. When all five are united, they will reveal the location to the greatest treasure on earth. To something so magnificent and powerful, the entire course of humanity will be forever altered. Now we have the ring and the compass, and the chalice has been with the Bauer family, right here at the castle, since the 1930s. A Nazi acquisition personally delivered to the castle by Heinrich Himmler, no less. He was lunched in this very room, not far from where you are standing, Dr Hunter. A fine man.'

'You have no shame at all, do you, Bauer?' Hunter said with contempt.

Bauer ignored his remark. 'These relics that you have wasted so much time and resources on trying to locate are all hidden away here in the castle, kept secret by a secret.' He smiled, revelling in the wordplay. 'The crucifix still eludes me, and as for the idol, I think we all know where that is.'

'Just one problem, Bauer,' Hunter said. 'Skulberg already searched the *Titanic* back in 1984. It's no dice. He couldn't find the idol anywhere.'

'Skulberg's dive in the eighties was a daring and partly successful adventure. But only partly successful. That is because, unfortunately for him, he didn't have this.'

Bauer pulled a letter from his suit jacket and passed it to Amy.

'It's a letter,' Amy said, quickly scanning the faded handwriting. 'Written by someone called George Wood. Some kind of confession. He says he and another man named Jeremiah Brown were paid to steal the idol and the ring from Skulberg for a man named Bauer. It's dated 1931. The Bauer he describes is your grandfather, Ernst. Am I right?'

Bauer's eyes crawled all over her. 'Yes, of course you are right, Agent Fox. I may be a powerful man, but the secret to immortality escapes me. The man referred to in the letter is my grandfather. He hired these pickpockets back in 1912 to steal two objects from Eirik Skulberg.'

'Let me guess, Skulberg's grandfather?' she asked.

'Right first time. As you can see, our two families go way back.'

'You mean, your family has been stealing from the Skulberg family for a long time.'

'I think we already covered that,' Bauer said. 'This letter, apparently written on Wood's deathbed in New York City and acquired by the Creed in the last few months, explains something that up until this time has been a mystery to both families, and anyone else with an interest in the matter. The thief Brown and his cohort told my grandfather that they stole the ring from Skulberg, but they were unable to get their hands on the idol. They handed the ring over, and my grandfather paid them half the fee as they had not fulfilled their part of the deal.'

Amy tutted. 'There's no honour among thieves.'

Bauer wandered away to a drinks cabinet and poured himself a glass of schnapps, one hand still in his suit pocket. 'My grandfather died on board the ship, going down right at the end with the captain, but before he died he sent a telegram explaining all of this to one of his associates. This is how we know part of the story. The rest is clarified in Wood's confession.'

A sip of schnapps. 'And both my grandfather's and Wood's story seemed to be proved when Skulberg launched his dive down to the *Titanic* back in the mid-eighties. He located my grandfather's quarters in first-class and, sure enough, found the compass and the ring, but only the compass and the ring. There was no sign of the idol. Now we know why. It went down to the bottom of the ocean with Jeremiah Brown in steerage.'

Amy nodded as she reached the bottom of the letter. 'He says here that when the chaos erupted on board, Jeremiah Brown went back to their berth to find it. He begged him to forget about it but he wouldn't listen. He died that night too, like Ernst Bauer, and the idol was lost forever.'

'Not forever.' Now, a grisly smile appeared on Bauer's face, and he gave a shallow nod of confirmation. 'Yes, it is my belief that the idol is down in steerage, in Brown and Wood's third-class bunk, exactly where it has rested since the night of the sinking.'

'And what do you intend to do about that?'

'Exactly what you are already thinking I am going to do. I intend to launch a salvage operation and dive down to the wreck. Once there, I will navigate to the precise location in steerage and locate the idol. Then I will have Skulberg's ring from Oslo, Woolf's compass from Las Vegas, the chalice from Heinrich Himmler, and the crucifix.'

'Wait,' Amy said. 'You know where that is too?'

'Yes, and you do not,' he said with a smirk. 'I will soon have both that and the idol itself, from the floor of the North Atlantic. Then, all five of de Gama's famous relics will be in my possession, as will the coordinates of what he found in the South American jungle.'

'And what is that?' Hunter asked.

Bauer went so still, it was almost as if time itself had stopped. The wind howled outside the castle windows. 'That is none of your concern, Dr Hunter. In fact, nothing is your concern now. You and the rest of your friends must sadly perish here tonight. While the rest of the world will surely know what de Gama stumbled upon, the five of you certainly will not. Now, isn't that ironic?'

Amy heard a young woman screaming. One of the armed men stormed into the room, dragging Quinn behind him.

'She was in a car outside the grounds. She was using this.' The man waved a mini laptop.

Bauer nodded. He knew. 'I guessed as much. Smash the computer.'

The man dropped the laptop to the floor with a clatter and stamped on it until it broke apart into dozens of pieces. Then he snatched up the hard drive. 'I'll throw this in the furnace.'

Quinn winced. 'That was my personal property, you asshole!'

Bauer said, 'The furnace is some distance away from this room, Agent Mosley. Considering your immediate fate, I dare say it will outlive you.'

'What are you talking about?' she asked, turning to Amy. 'What does he mean?'

Bauer was lost in thought, his eyes glazed over as he dreamed of de Gama's mysterious treasure. 'No, I have said enough.' He walked over to the door and swung it open. 'Zeller, the rug.'

The Austrian commando padded into the room, leaned over and grabbed the Persian rug. When he dragged it over to one side, it revealed something that turned Amy's blood to ice.

14

A trapdoor, just like the one they had seen back in the Bavarian castle.

She stared at it in horror. It was made of old, tarnished wood, and the patches of bubbling rust bit at the black, iron hinges. From somewhere far beneath it, she now heard a low, deep growl and the sound of something very heavy shifting position. Their host walked over to the trapdoor and kicked at one of the hinges with the toe of his shoe and smiled to himself.

'What the hell are you keeping down there?' she asked, almost breathless with fear.

Bauer nodded as if he understood her pain like a disinterested doctor. 'When people ask me that question, Agent Fox, I usually reply with something along the lines of "your worst fears", but in your case, I'm happy to expand. Deep down in the darkness below this room is a suite of rooms the layman might call a dungeon. In this place, the Creed houses one of its most prized possessions. You see, after you attacked Black Rock Castle, this possession had to be transported somewhere safer. We at Schloss Kapfenstein were very proud to be given such a high honour. Here, inside these great, ancient stone walls, we call this possession the Chimäre.'

'The Chimera?' Hunter said. 'That's not possible.'

Bauer strolled across the room towards his antique cocktail cabinet, carefully walking around the trapdoor on his way. 'Why ever not?'

'Because the Chimera was part of Greek mythology, not history,' Hunter countered. 'That's why not. It was created by Homer for his epic "Iliad" poem. A fire-breathing monster created from the parts of various beasts, most usually described as part lion, part goat, and part snake. Myth.'

Bauer poured another schnapps and waved the bottle at Amy. 'Will you join me?'

'I'd be disgusted to share a drink with a man like you. That's your answer.'

His face hardened. He drank some schnapps and glanced momentarily at the trapdoor. 'I think you should watch your tongue.'

She took a step back. Hunter stepped up beside her and said, 'I don't like men who threaten women, Bauer.'

'I'm equally as happy to threaten you. Shut your mouth or I will have you fed to the Chimera.'

Quinn took a step back behind Blanco. Jodie's eyes narrowed, burning with hate.

'I'll see you dead and buried under the ground, Bauer,' Hunter said. 'Count on it.'

The Austrian was unmoved by the comment. He seemed almost to enjoy it. 'Your choice, but you really should have joined me in a drink, Agent Fox. It is the very finest my country has to offer, but then I'm biased. You see, this particular schnapps is distilled right here in Schloss Kapfenstein – not from grain but only from the very best ripe pears and with water from a totally pure mountain stream running through the grounds. You are missing out on a rare experience, and so shortly before your death as well. It seems a shame.'

Hunter bristled at the Austrian's attitude. 'She said no, Bauer.'

'Ah, the archaeologist speaks again. Let's hope your knowledge of ancient pots and pans is better than your knowledge of Greek mythology.'

They all heard the creature shift position below the room once again, and another long, low rumble echoed up through the trapdoor.

'Despite its recent meal, it gets hungry often.' Bauer pressed a button on his drinks cabinet and called another man into the room. The door swung open to reveal a man dressed as a butler. He walked past Zeller and tipped his head to Bauer.

Bauer said, 'Schweighofer, it's time to show our guests exactly how much of an appetite our beautiful one down there can build up.'

'Yes, sir.'

Schweighofer clicked his heels and bowed and then left through the open door. With the sound of heels tapping on the stone floor echoing into the room, Bauer turned once more, schnapps glass in hand, and strolled back over to them, again taking care not to step on the trapdoor.

'What do you mean, despite its recent meal?' Hunter asked.

'Two men I employed to get me the compass in Las Vegas. Their names were Ferrari and Axelrod. When they delivered the compass, they thought they might try to blackmail more money out of me for it. They even drew guns on me. Can you imagine the nerve of it? Anyway, they presented little challenge to the power of the Creed. I had Zeller and his men disarm them and throw them into this pit.'

Amy covered her mouth, working hard not to throw up. 'My God, you're a psychopath.'

Bauer's facial expression didn't flicker. 'It was a mistake for your team to come here tonight,' he said coldly. 'Your fate, of course, was sealed after clashing with us in the hunt for Atlantis, but to come right here into the heart of our network in the search for de Gama's five sacred objects was a big mistake. You have failed to achieve your mission objective, unless that objective was to expedite your own deaths. That has certainly been achieved tonight, but first, we have other business to attend to.'

Schweighofer returned at the head of a column of six men, all dressed in long robes with hoods over their heads, partially obscuring their faces. Some robes were black, some brown and one at the back was purple. The one wearing the purple robe was carrying a white robe, which he now gave to Bauer with a solemn bow of the head.

Bauer slammed his schnapps down his throat and set the glass down before donning the robe. For a few seconds, nothing but the sound of the rustling fabric of the robes could be heard as the men gathered in a semi-circle around the trapdoor. Hunter, Amy, and the rest of the team now watched in disbelief as two armed men dragged a gagged and bound woman into the room. In the low candlelight, they saw her desperate eyes staring at the hooded figures in horror. Then those eyes crawled over to the HARPA team, standing at gunpoint in the corner. They heard her grunt in fear as the men forced her to her feet. Hunter recognised the woman, but couldn't place her.

Bauer smiled. 'Thank you, gentlemen. Open the trapdoor.'

One of the men unlocked the padlock and slid back the two heavy bolts. Then he gripped the grab-handle and heaved the heavy wooden door up and over. It landed with a heavy thud on the old Persian rug and made the gagged woman jump in shock. A stink of rotting meat and dung filled the room.

Bauer turned and spoke to the HARPA team. 'Meet Viktoria Brenner, a former high-ranking official of the Creed.' As an afterthought, he added, 'Oh yes, she was also the Austrian culture minister up until two years ago.'

Now Hunter got it. He'd seen her deliver a lecture on sites of archaeological interest in the European Union during his time at UNESCO. Something about her former fame and high profile made what he was watching even more sordid and shocking than it might otherwise have been.

'Frau Brenner made the unfortunate mistake of leaking certain key secrets held securely by the Creed for centuries to the BVT – the Bundesamt für Verfassungsschutz und Terrorismusbekämpfung – or in English, the Office for the Protection of the Constitution and Counterterrorism. This, naturally, was another big error of judgement.' He turned to one of the men holding the struggling woman. 'Gag, Posch.'

A man with tattoos on his arm roughly pulled the gag out of her mouth. It came to rest around her neck like a choker as she gasped for air. 'Please, Magus!'

Hunter and Amy stared at each other. So, Bauer was the Magus that Adler, the Teacher, had been serving during the race to Atlantis. He turned and saw from the look on his friends' faces that they had been just as shocked to learn this as he and Amy. As the shock registered on their faces, the sombre men and women in robes took up their positions around the trapdoor.

'Please!' Brenner continued, panicked when she saw the robed people gather around the trapdoor. 'It wasn't me! I never gave the BVT a thing, not a single piece of paper or a single email. Nothing! Someone else inside the Creed has betrayed you. You have a traitor in your midst, Dear Magus! Killing me will not solve your problem.'

'There is no point in begging, Viktoria,' Bauer said. 'I know it was you. I always knew it was you. I am everywhere. I am the Magus of the Creed. I know everything. Just last night I was sitting downstairs in the grand conference room with the owners of every newspaper and TV station in the West, informing them of the editorial narrative they will take during the upcoming crisis in the United States.'

'What crisis?' Amy asked. 'There is no crisis.'

He smiled. 'Not yet, no. The accident hasn't happened yet, but we are not here to discuss the Creed's intimate business details. We are here to observe a very solemn ritual – the ritual we must follow when our most sacred trust is broken by one of those closest to us. As I believe you already know, the Creed was established when European high society banned the Illuminati. Now, the burden of controlling the direction of this world rests on our shoulders alone. It is a heavy burden, made even weightier when one of our own turns on us.'

'I did no such thing!' Brenner screamed. 'I already told you – it was not me! You have a traitor in your ranks, Magus. A filthy traitor!'

'You are the traitor,' Bauer said, his face still mostly obscured by the white hood. 'Like all of us here, you were invited into our fold because of your ancient bloodline, and yet you have betrayed your own blood by passing some of our secrets to the authorities.'

'No!'

'Take her to the edge, Hackl.'

'Yes, sir.'

Then, without pausing or consideration, the man Bauer had ordered grabbed the trembling woman roughly by the shoulders and dragged her over to the pit's entrance.

15

Brenner screamed a terrible, bloodcurdling roar. 'No! Please!'

'Confess to your crimes and I will have you shot before you go into the pit. You have seen what happens to people who go down there alive, Viktoria. Think it over carefully.'

Tears ran down from her bulging, terrified eyes. Her chest heaved up and down. She stared down into the black pit and tried to scream again. Instead, she passed out and went limp in the men's arms.

'Zeller! Bring her around.' Bauer turned to face Hunter and the team. 'You will see what happens to people who cross the Creed, and in your case just minutes before you suffer the same fate. Perhaps you should argue over who goes into the pit after Viktoria Brenner. The winner goes first. As my beautiful beast grows less hungry, it keeps its victims alive longer. Plays cat and mouse with them. Believe me when I tell you that down in that place' – he paused and raised his white-robed arm towards the pit – 'it is better to die fast.'

'You are one sick bastard,' Jodie said. 'You know that?'

'The opinion of a lowly car thief and cat burglar from a poor part of California means about as much to me as you might guess it does.'

'You're an animal!' Lewis said. 'And that's the opinion of a US Marine.'

'No, the Chimera is an animal, and you will soon learn the difference. I am a sophisticated human being with taste and class. The cream of the cream. I am courted by presidents and prime ministers and princes. The Chimera is not only an animal, but an animal that might choose to rip your leg off and then cauterise the wound with its fiery breath just to keep its meat supply fresh for a few more days while it eats your leg in front of you. If you don't watch your tone, Agent Lewis, I'll see to it you go down last so you can enjoy that experience.'

Horrified by what she had just heard, Amy turned and vomited on the floor. Jodie ran over to her and put her arm around her shoulders, wheeling her away from Bauer and towards the narrow embrasure window a few steps behind them.

Bauer was unmoved and turned quietly to his butler. 'Schweighofer, please have some of the staff clean this mess up after the ritual.'

'Sir.'

Brenner was slowly regaining consciousness in the soldiers' arms. When she came to, she remembered where she was and screamed until the tattooed soldier clamped his hand over her mouth.

'If you want the bullet,' Bauer said coldly, 'confess and repent.'

The soldier removed his hand.

'Then yes! I gave the BVT the information. It was me. Please, don't throw me down there alive, Magus! I beg you to please shoot me dead first!'

'Good, very good. You have surprised and impressed me with your honesty. But I want you to know your treachery was all for nothing. You asked too many questions when you were inducted into our fold and raised some suspicion. The secrets you were given were pieces of false information we gave to you on purpose to see if you would leak it. Only you had this information and that is how we knew you were the traitor. The authorities learned nothing about us but lies, and you exposed yourself as a traitor for nothing.'

'But—'

'Feed the beast!'

'No!' she said, struggling and screaming in the soldiers' arms. 'You said you would shoot me first! Please, Magus! I beg you!'

'And you swore the sacred Creed oath. Tonight, we all shall see what happens to traitors. Goodbye, Minister Brennan.'

'No! No! Please... no!'

The men hurled her into the pit, hands still tied behind her back, and she landed with a crunch on the floor. The beast's response was instant. Its growl was so low and loud it shook the bolts on the trapdoor. Brenner's screaming turned to whimpers. They heard her feet shuffling in the dirt as she backed up against the circular pit wall.

'They all do that,' Bauer said, peering over the edge. 'Better to throw yourself into its jaws. You men, close the trapdoor.'

Even the soldiers were paling as they walked over and closed the door. Those in robes took a step back, still eerily silent. Now, Brennan screamed again, but this time in the dark. Amy was shaking. Blanco moved in front of her and Jodie. Lewis and Hunter were at the front, the Londoner doing his best to control himself and not give away the fear he felt pounding through every sinew in his body.

Another roar.

A scream and a flash of bright light around the edges of the trapdoor.

'It breathes its fire!' Bauer said.

The hooded men and women bowed their heads and clasped their hands together in some kind of coordinated ritual movement. Hunter's mind was still racing, almost in total denial, as he was forced to watch such a vile ritual murder. He heard the woman screaming and crying and then they all heard the beast growling and scratching and biting, and another flash of fiery light exploded in the pit. Smoke drifted up through the gaps in the trapdoor and then they heard the sound of bones cracking and an eerie crunching noise down in the darkness. Brenner made no more noise.

'Goddamn this!' Hunter said. 'You're depraved, Bauer!'

'And you're next. Swoboda, Albrecht! Bring Dr Hunter to the trapdoor. The beast will be done with Brenner in another minute or so.'

Amy screamed. 'No! Stop this!'

'Say goodbye to your friends, Dr Hunter,' Bauer said with a smile. 'And pray you die fast as Veronika Brenner did. Open the trapdoor!'

16

As the soldiers dragged him across the room to the trapdoor, Hunter was getting the impression that he and Bauer weren't exactly hitting it off. Now, it looked like he was rapidly running out of time to make a better impression. He knew he had to move fast.

He broke free from the men and launched himself across the room, striking Bauer with the full force of his right fist and knocking him to the floor. Hunter's attack was so fast and unexpected, the Magus landed with a bone-crunching thud and a look of surprise and terror on his face. When he saw the archaeologist padding over to him to finish the job, he screamed at the other men and women to fight back. Then he rolled twice and leaped to his feet, reaching out and swiping a crucifix from the top of the cocktail cabinet.

Team HARPA engaged in a battle against the soldiers and robed strangers. Confronted with Bauer and his crucifix, Hunter never flinched. With the sound of chaotic fighting all around him, he lunged forward a second time, smacking the heavy gold crucifix from Bauer's hand and tackling him to the floor once again. This time he took care to pin the Magus down and wrenched his arm up towards his shoulder blades, forcing an agonised scream out of him.

Behind him, Jodie was fighting one of the women in the white robes. After delivering a hard smack with the back of her hand, she jumped up onto the dais behind the woman, spun around, and extended her leg, kicking her opponent in the face with her boot. To her left, Blanco struck out at a soldier, two rapid and heavy-hitting blows to the chest and a third in his throat, which crushed his windpipe and instantly ended the fight.

Many of the white robes had fled in the chaos, and Lewis and Jodie had taken care of those who chose to stay in the fight. After the young Marine had disarmed the last soldier and knocked him out, Hunter was now the only man engaged in the fight, still struggling with Bauer himself. The Austrian looked weak but turned out to have some chops. Hunter recognised the moves as some kind of martial art, but the ex-soldier was younger and fitter than his opponent.

After ducking a tiger punch, Hunter managed to land two fast punches in Bauer's stomach and forced him to double over. Then he brought his knee up and piled it into his face, blasting him back against the cabinet and knocking over a large candelabra. Flames instantly caught hold of a tapestry behind the cabinet and began to lick up the wall.

'We have to go,' he said. 'We haven't got long to find what we need before this entire place goes up.'

'Where do we start?' Amy said.

'I'd start here.' Hunter reached down, grabbed the letter Bauer had shown Amy, and pulled a ring off his finger. 'I saw it as soon as we walked in here. Identical to the image Skulberg showed us.'

'Damn it, Hunter,' Jodie said. 'I hate it when you're good.'

'In that case, you must be a very hateful person.'

'What about the compass?' Lewis said.

'And the chalice,' said Amy. 'He said Himmler delivered a chalice to the Creed back in the thirties.'

'The obvious place to start is a safe,' Blanco said, coughing as the smoke began to collect in a fat cushion below the ceiling. 'But we don't have long as Max says, and we need to find it first.' Behind him, the flames were devouring the drapes and crawling up to the ceiling.

'This is his study, so let's try the drawing room,' Hunter said.

'Wait,' Amy cried out, pointing at the trapdoor. 'What about that thing?'

They paused. No one knew what to do. Then, Blanco drew his gun and walked over to the open trapdoor. Firing blindly into the darkness, he emptied his magazine. They all heard the roars and cries of anguish and pain from deep below, then silence.

'You think that did it?' Jodie asked.

Blanco grabbed her arm and ran to the door. 'I think it's too late to worry about it.'

'What if there's more than one?' Quinn said. 'What if they have one in another room? He said there was a whole dungeon down there.'

'We can worry about all that later!' Amy said.

Leaving Bauer's unconscious body on the rug, they fled the burning room, and Hunter led them down the hall the way they had come and then back down the stairs.

'This is our last chance,' said Amy, coughing in the smoke. 'After that, it could be anywhere.'

Hunter stepped inside the old drawing room. He found an ornate, luxurious room fully furnished with mostly seventeenth and eighteenth-century chairs and tables. A velvet chaise longue, gilded with gold leaf, sparkled on another Persian rug in the centre of the room. Jodie wandered inside, her footsteps muffled by the thick goat wool of the rug.

Hunter and Blanco were already taking the chaise longue off the rug, while Lewis stood guard at the door with Quinn.

'I didn't think places like this really existed,' Jodie said, gawping at the diamond chandelier.

'Oh yeah, they sure do,' Amy said. 'But we can't stop to admire the opulence. We need to find de Gama's relics before Bauer's men regroup and come to find us. Any luck?'

Hunter and Blanco had nearly finished moving the chaise longue off the rug. 'Someone give me a hand! We need to pull this rug back and see if there's a floor safe. They're the hidey-hole of choice for people in Bauer's income bracket.'

'Yeah, I think he made that point with the damn trapdoor upstairs,' Quinn said.

Jodie made her way across the room and helped Hunter and Blanco lift the large antique chair away from the rug. Then Blanco and the Englishman walked to opposite corners of it, pushed it over, and began to roll it up out of the way. When the job was done, Amy stood with her hands on her hips and sighed.

'No floor safe,' she said. 'Bummer.'

'No,' said Hunter. 'Which is a shame, because I'd have looked really clever.'

'Don't give up on that goal just yet, Hunter,' Jodie said as she brushed past him on her way to a bookcase on the far side of the room. 'Remember – there's a first time for everything.'

He gave her a look, and Lewis, who was guarding the door with his gun drawn, gave his trademark chuckle. 'She's too fast for you, Max. Admit it.'

Hunter said nothing. Seeing Jodie and Quinn were now both searching the bookcase at the far end of the room, and Blanco and Amy were at work rifling through some antique cabinets on the adjacent wall, he decided to remove a series of impressive oil paintings from the walls.

'Not giving up on the safe idea, right?' Amy said with a glance over her shoulder.

Hunter raised his eyebrows but made no reply, determined to find Bauer's stash before anyone else in the room. After he'd removed three of the heavy paintings, he sighed.

'Starting to get the picture?' Jodie said.

'Funny,' he said, lifting the final painting from the wall.

'Still no safe, huh?' Quinn said, seeing he'd drawn another blank. 'Maybe you're running out of luck after all.'

'But I'm not,' Amy said. 'Look what I just found in a hidden compartment inside this cabinet.' She held a crumbling manuscript up in the candlelight. Beside it was a wooden cylinder wrapped in crumbling parchment, scrawled with strange symbols. 'An old manuscript, but what the hell is this thing?'

Hunter cast a quick eye over it. 'I don't know, but it looks old and important.'

Jodie rolled her eyes. 'And that's your professional opinion?'

'Until I get some Alone Time with it, it'll have to do. And we still need the damned chalice and compass, too.'

'They could be anywhere,' Jodie said.

Hunter snapped his fingers. 'Not anywhere. Damn it! How could I have been so stupid? I know where they are!'

17

'Remember when Bauer said that the compass and Himmler's chalice were hidden by the secret of secrets?'

'Yeah, I thought that was weird,' Amy said.

Hunter said, 'Not so weird when you know who Harpocrates is.'

'Damn it again,' Jodie said.

Hunter winked. 'Sorry, but yeah. Follow me.'

Ahead of them was the main door where Zeller and his men had brought them inside the castle, but Hunter led them off to the right and across the main hall. The smoke was thicker now and getting more dangerous by the second, but still largely restricted to the upper floors. Then they heard men shouting and footsteps on the staircase.

'This way!' Hunter called out as they stepped into a room in the east wing. 'I saw it when we walked past earlier. It meant nothing at the time, not until our host referred to the secret of secrets. Behold!'

He pointed to a large oil painting of a young boy, classical in style, holding a finger to his lips.

'An Egyptian?' Amy asked.

'No, it's Harpocrates, the ancient Greek god of silence and secrets.'

Jodie stepped towards it, mesmerised by its beauty. 'Then why is he wearing that Egyptian headdress thing?'

'It's called a nemes,' said Hunter. 'And he's wearing it because the

Greeks stole him from Egyptian theology. His Egyptian name is Hr-fi-hrd. He's mentioned in the Pyramid Texts with the name Horus-the-Child with the Finger in his Mouth. He keeps the secrets, and in this case, I'm betting the big secret is a safe behind his painting. C'mon!'

As Blanco tore down the painting, they all saw Hunter was right. A small, steel safe was neatly embedded in the plaster behind the painting.

'Et voila!' Hunter said.

'But how do we get inside?' asked Quinn.

Blanco pushed Hunter aside, reaching into his bag. 'Brute force, spelled D.Y.N.A.M.I.T.E. It also spells: stand back, kids.'

Nobody needed asking twice. Taking cover at the back of the room by upturning a heavy wooden table, they watched as Blanco worked fast, opening his pack, then fitting some dynamite just in front of the safe door. Trailing a detonator cord behind him, he scrambled over to them.

'All ready?'

Before anyone answered, he hit the detonator. The blast was hard and deep, instantly filling the room with yet more smoke and debris, mostly from the enormous hole now blown out the wall where the safe had once been.

Coughing in the smoke as they broke cover, Quinn spoke first. 'I see a giant hole where the safe was, but no safe.'

'It's over here,' Amy said. 'Behind the couch.'

'Did we do it?' said Hunter.

'Of course we did.' Blanco looked at Amy expectantly. 'Right?'

'Right. We have one compass once belonging to Francisco de Gama and this little baby...' She held up a shining, golden chalice, covered in dust and filth. Embedded with sparkling diamonds and sapphires and rubies and emeralds, it was astonishingly beautiful. 'You think this is it?'

Hunter's mouth fell open. 'Er... yeah, I think it just might be!'

Lewis, who was watching the corridor from the door, had turned into the room and was staring at the chalice in amazement. 'Holy cow, that thing is awesome.'

'The corridor, Ben!' Amy said. 'You can admire the antiques later!'

'Sorry,' he said, smiling and turning back to keep watch. 'But damn...'

Hunter walked over to Amy and took in the chalice. Blanco, Jodie, and

Quinn gathered around too, each staring at the gold and jewels twinkling in the candlelight.

'Whoa,' Jodie said. 'That has to be worth a few bucks.'

Blanco nodded. 'It sure is a grand-looking thing all right.'

Quinn shrugged. 'Meh. It's a little too baroque for my taste. I'm more of a modernist.'

Hunter's eyes had left the chalice and turned to Amy. 'We need to get out of here. Now.'

'And you can forget about the SUV,' Quinn said. 'After Zeller dragged me out of it, his men turned it into a mesh strainer. Then it exploded.'

Hunter frowned. 'Helpful.'

Amy ran a hand through her hair, desperation in her eyes. 'Yeah, just… great.'

'We can worry about that later,' Hunter said. 'This whole place is going to be collapsing in the fire any second. The walls might be able to stand the blaze, but the roof beams cannot. We need to go! Now!'

They sprinted outside into the courtyard. Hearing a man screaming, they looked up to the roof and saw Bauer in the blizzard, staggering along the balustrade, coughing and lurching all over the place. Behind him, Zeller and some other men spotted them and opened fire, peppering the courtyard with bullets.

Team HARPA scattered in all directions. Hunter and Amy found safety behind the wall dividing the main entrance from the courtyard, but Blanco, Lewis and Quinn were too far ahead and ran for the main turret. Jodie was halfway in between and in danger. She broke away to her left and ran towards the castle's western wall.

Amy watched her run with terrified eyes. 'She's not going to make it!'

Hunter laid down some heavy cover fire. Blanco and Lewis did the same, driving Bauer's forces on the roof back away from the edge and ending the attack. Jodie reached the western wall and ran up an exposed staircase until she reached the top where she ducked down behind a low crenelated wall for cover, drawing her gun.

'Shit, that was a little too close,' she said over the comms.

Amy breathed a sigh of relief. 'Way too close. Can you make it down to the—'

Her words were terminated by the silhouette of a large black helicopter looming over the wall behind Jodie.

'Bauer's escaping!'

'No, I don't think so,' said Blanco over the comms. 'Our new friends in the chopper are firing on Bauer across the courtyard!'

He was right, the chopper's chin-mounted machinegun now opened fire on Bauer and his men as they scrambled over the roof tiles. The rounds cut many of his men down, but Bauer and Zeller were at the front and had just enough time to jump somewhere out of sight. After a few more of Bauer's men joined them, the chopper descended over the western wall and disappeared from sight. Then it rose up again, further along the wall near to Jodie's position.

Amy watched the next minute unfold in a grim, slow-motion nightmare. A rope ladder tumbled out of the hovering aircraft and a man in black combat fatigues slid down it in seconds. She watched Jodie try and find cover behind the western turret. A short exchange of fire. Guns kicking back with recoil, smoke puffing out of muzzles before being caught by the wind. Jodie's handgun was no match for the man's semi-automatic machine pistol.

'Jodie, hang on!' Amy cried out into the comms. 'I'm coming to get you.'

'It's over,' Jodie said. 'I can't hold out any more.'

Amy jumped on the comms. 'Just keep it up for another few seconds, damn it! We're on our way!'

'I said it's over, Amy!' Jodie's voice was cold and angry. 'You guys have to get the hell away from here while you still can.'

Amy moved to scramble out of her cover position, but Hunter grabbed her arm and stopped her.

'What are you doing?' she said angrily. 'We have to get over there and help her!'

He shook his head and pointed over her shoulder. When she saw the transport helicopter rising from the castle roof, she knew what had happened. Jodie's face was just visible inside one of the rear windows, sad and scared. Then the aircraft rotated in the heavy snow and sped away, quickly disappearing inside the low cloud ceiling.

Over the comms, they heard Jodie shouting at someone, and then a rustling sound. 'You're hurting me!' Jodie said. 'Let go of my wrist!'

Then, a hard, cold voice. A man's voice. 'Don't come after us, Team HARPA. We have Agent Priest. She is our insurance policy against any further interventions by you. Any attempt to follow us or thwart our plans will result in her immediate execution.'

The comms went dead.

Static.

After a long, stunned silence, Amy said. 'We're getting her back, right now.'

'You bet we are,' said Blanco. 'So let's get on with it.'

18

'This is looking even more complicated than when we started,' Amy said. She was still pale in the face but the trembling had finally stopped. She was holding a bottle of beer in her hand and now she took a long, slow sip. She put the bottle back on the little cardboard beermat and sighed. 'Much more complicated. Poor Jodie. I feel so responsible.'

'We just have more information than before,' Quinn said with a calm shrug. 'And more information is always good.'

Amy drank more beer. 'It's not like you to be so glass-half-full.'

The young goth shrugged again, this time more self-consciously as everyone was looking at her. 'Just saying, is all.'

The team was gathered around a table inside Innsbruck's Paninothek cocktail bar on Adamgasse, in the heart of the ancient city. The place was busy but the talk was mostly reserved and quiet. On their table, their drinks formed a circle around a large pizza-in-teglia loaded with cheese, mushrooms, and basil. Trying but failing to wind down in the relaxed ambiance, Blanco leaned forward and helped himself to another slice.

'Jodie is our priority now, and Quinn's right,' he said. 'More information is always good. We just have to process it, that's all. Make sense of it. We have the ring, the compass the chalice, and this weird manuscript. We also know there's a good chance Bauer and Zeller and some of his men are still alive. And now we also know there's another player in the game. Whoever snatched Jodie also just happened to want to cut Bauer and his goons to pieces with a serious machinegun.'

'That's the part that worries me most,' Amy said. 'God, I hope Jodie's all right.'

'What does the expert think?' Lewis said, turning to Hunter.

'What bothers me is that there was no sign of McCabe back at the castle,' Hunter said.

'What are you thinking?' Amy asked.

'That maybe he was in the chopper?' said Blanco. 'That's what I was thinking.'

'Maybe, maybe not,' said Hunter. 'Whoever was in the helicopter tried to murder Bauer, who is Creed, and we know McCabe works for the Creed. So unless it was an inter-factional scrap, I doubt Brodie was on board that chopper.'

'So, what about the relics?' Amy asked. 'Any luck with them?'

'They have strange inscriptions on them,' he said, still rubbing his jaw from the fight back up in the castle. 'I think I need some help, is what I think.'

'The great Dr Max Hunter needs some help?' Amy said. 'Did I just hear that right?'

'The deeper you go, the narrower things get,' said Hunter.

Quinn had to struggle not to spit out her beer. 'What?'

'In research,' Hunter said, managing to keep his smile hidden from the table. 'As you progress through an academic career, your field of knowledge generally becomes much deeper, but the price you pay for this is that it also becomes narrower. I can tell you right now that the symbols on these old objects that once belonged to our fifteenth-century explorer de Gama mean absolutely nothing to me at all. They're not Egyptian, Greek, Latin... not Hindu, Arabic, you name it. I just can't tell you what they mean.'

'What do you suggest, then?' Amy asked.

Hunter leaned back in his chair, sipped his beer, and gave a short sigh. 'I'm the last person to admit defeat, but I suggest we show them to Juliette Bonnaire at UNESCO. Her knowledge is much broader than mine, and if she doesn't know what they are, she'll know someone who does. I'll give her a call and see if...'

His phone rang. He looked down and saw the caller ID. 'Well, that's weird.'

'What's weird?' Quinn asked.

'It's Juliette Bonnaire. Talk of the devil and all that.'

Amy and Blanco shared a worried glance. 'See what she wants,' Amy said.

Hunter had already answered the phone. 'Juliette, *bonsoir*.'

'It's a good job that castle wasn't a UNESCO listed site, no?' said the Frenchwoman sharply.

He sighed. 'It's good to hear your sweet voice again. I was just about to call you and... Wait a minute. How do you know about the castle?'

'When I tell you, you will not believe me. How soon can you get to Paris?'

He looked at his watch. 'We have a private jet, but it has to be refuelled and the pilot has to file a flight plan. Still, you're only an hour or so away. We could be there before midnight.'

'*Bon*,' Juliette said tartly. 'Don't be late, and put your thinking hat on, Max. You're going to need it, and so will Agent Jodie Priest.'

19

When Hunter settled down in the chair opposite Juliette Bonnaire, he couldn't have felt more at home even with a pipe and slippers. The nighttime view of the Paris skyline out of the window behind her desk was unchanged and as beautiful as ever and she was even wearing the same old Chanel perfume she always wore.

Juliette smiled at him from behind the desk and relaxed in her chair. *'Qu'on est bien chez soi... non?'*

'Peut-être,' he said, returning her smile. *'Je voulais te parler de ça.'*

She raised an eyebrow, but Amy spoke first. 'Is this a conversation anyone can join? If so, then maybe we'd better have it in a language we all understand.'

'Sorry,' Hunter said. 'That was rude of me.'

'And now the great Max Hunter is apologising?' Quinn said, turning to Amy. 'Do you housetrain feral dogs, too?'

'We're not here to talk about Max's career, apologies, or feral dogs,' Juliette said, losing the smile by the time she reached the end of the sentence. 'We are here because of what happened to you in Austria and what happened to me shortly before I called you there.'

'You need to know that Jodie was kidnapped,' Hunter said.

'This I already know.'

He turned from his former boss to Amy. She looked as confused as he felt. 'How do you know about that? No one on the team has told you about Jodie.'

'Why not find out for yourself?' Juliette said, leaning forward and pressing a button on her desk phone. 'Luckily, I had the presence of mind to record the call as soon as my suspicions were raised.' A second later, they all heard a deep man's voice speaking with a Spanish accent.

'Professor Bonnaire, your reputation precedes you.'

'Who is this?'

'You do not need to know this. All you need to do is listen. First, we have Agent Jodie Priest from the HARPA Team. Second, we want the artifacts that the team recently liberated from the Creed at Schloss Kapfenstein. Third, we propose a simple trade. Priest's life for the artifacts. No tricks on either side or she dies.'

'I will need to call them,' Juliette's voice said.

'Do what you have to. Just make it happen.'

'You said the HARPA team took the objects from the Creed.'

'Yes.'

'Then, who are you?'

He laughed. 'Someone who hates the Creed even more than you do.'

'Is that it?'

'No,' his cool, low voice said. 'The Creed knew the location of de Gama's fourth relic. I expect the HARPA team to determine where this was, to retrieve it, and then to bring it to us as part of the trade. I will expect you to contact me within forty-eight hours. This is more than generous and enough time for them to find what I want. You will order Team HARPA to search for the fourth relic and then they will trade all four of the relics with us, or Agent Priest will be executed.'

The line was abruptly cut.

Amy looked like she was going to be sick. 'Who the hell was that?'

Juliette shrugged. 'As of right now, I have no idea. I wanted to speak with all of you before contacting the police.'

'Good thinking,' Hunter said. 'We don't know anything about this latest guy. He could be very unpredictable. We need to put our heads together and really think carefully about this before making our next move.'

'But we know so little,' Amy said.

Juliette frowned. 'Let's start with what you do know. Tell me about this

Bauer. Maybe we can find something in his backstory that might indicate who this new man is.'

'His full name is Hans Eberhard Bauer,' Amy said. 'And thanks to Agent Mosley and the research she conducted on the flight from Innsbruck, I can now give everyone a little more information about him. He was born in Vienna in the late 1940s. His father was a government official, starting his career in the First Austrian Republic and ending it after the Anschluss. That was back in March 1938 when the Nazis annexed Austria to create what they called a Greater Germany.'

Juliette added, 'The process called the Anschluss means the union.'

Amy went on. 'And according to Quinn's digging, Bauer's father worked for the Nazis during this time.'

'Which explains the Himmler connection,' said Hunter.

'Right. Bauer was basically a full collaborator with the Nazi Party but unlike a number of other high-ranking Austrian Nazis, he didn't flee the country for Argentina at the end of the war via the rat lines.'

'Why not?' Blanco asked.

'Because he was Creed,' Quinn said from the back of the room. 'That's why. He was a senior Creed figure and so were many of the most senior American, British and French Allies who set up the new governments in Germany and Austria after the war.'

Amy said, 'Basically, Creed membership was more important to these people than their national status or whatever war crimes they committed during the war. Franz-Josef Bauer was able to use his secret society membership to wriggle out of his part in the war and went on to live a very fruitful and interesting life after the war as a businessman. His Creed membership guaranteed several lucrative contracts with US importers after the war and it was around then he met and married a woman from Graz. Hans Bauer was born shortly after and immediately inherited the bloodline and Creed membership at his birth. The fortune came later when his father passed away during the 1980s.'

'And now he's the Magus,' Lewis said. 'But do any of us really know what that even means?'

'Not really,' said Amy. 'From our interaction with Karl Adler – The Teacher – during the Atlantis mission, we know the Magus is a very senior figure in the Creed, most likely the very highest. As such, he'll be responsible for their global management. How many underlings he has, controlling the world's different regions, is something we just do not know.'

'But I think we have enough to be going on with,' Hunter said. 'Bauer is the Magus and after his failure to secure Atlantis he seems to have set his sights on another prize which has something to do with de Gama's five sacred golden relics. If we knew what that was, we'd be a hell of a lot better off than we currently are.'

'Unfortunately, we have two big problems on that score,' Blanco said. 'First, we only have three of the five objects, and second, we have no idea how to decipher the code de Gama carved into them.'

'Quite,' Juliette said. 'What about this fourth artifact the man mentioned in the phone call?'

It was Amy's turn to shrug. 'Search me. We have only the ring, the compass, and the chalice.'

'That's not all we have,' Hunter said, reaching into his old army bag. 'We also have a manuscript and this weird little wooden cylinder, which we found inside Bauer's bijou little residence back in the mountains.'

Juliette raised an eyebrow. 'Looks fascinating, and the manuscript looks very old.'

'Some of it's older than other parts. I think there's a good chance part of it may be in de Gama's own handwriting, but I'm not an expert in that area. Other parts are much newer – some almost contemporary to our own era. It's written in Latin, Spanish, and German. I've had a crack at some of the Spanish, and I found the words *anillo de oro*, *brújula*, *cáliz*, *crucifio* and *ídolo* at various important sections of the text. These are the words for ring, compass, chalice, crucifix, and idol. We know the idol is the fifth relic – at least the way we're numbering them. I'm betting the crucifix is relic number four.'

'Is that what you were doing at the back of the plane?' Lewis asked, impressed.

'And I thought you were on the toilet the whole time,' said Quinn.

'No, that was just for part of the time,' Hunter said. 'But don't worry, I continued to work on the translation while I was on the job.'

Quinn looked disgusted. 'Nice.'

'I'm also betting,' Hunter continued, 'that the location of the fourth relic is in this manuscript someplace, or maybe this weird wooden cylinder might have some answers on that score, too.'

'Good old mindless optimism,' Juliette said. 'The same old Max I have always loved so.'

Hunter smiled. 'Thing is, part of the manuscript is written in some other language I simply do not recognize and have seen nowhere else in the world, except one place.'

'Where?' Juliette asked.

'The three artifacts we already have in our possession. The unknown language in the manuscript looks identical to that carved into those relics. Unfortunately, this is where my genius runs out.'

Amy shook her head. 'And modest, too.'

'Have no fear,' Juliette said. 'I already predicted the limits of your genius, Max. This is why I have recalled a specialist in the field to fly to Paris immediately and study the symbols on the objects you have secured.'

'A symbologist?' Quinn asked.

Juliette and Hunter both winced.

'Yes, but we're not going to call them that,' Juliette said. 'Because there is no such word. We're going to call this person a semiotician because that is what we call people who decipher symbols.'

'Touched a raw nerve?' asked Quinn.

'Not at all, but I just hate that word. Anyway, we move on. Unfortunately, my expert is in Cambodia at this time, working on a very exciting discovery recently found at Angkor Wat, another very famous UNESCO World Heritage Site. They cannot be here until tomorrow evening, and it's very good of them to fly back at such short notice. Until they get a good look at the compass, ring and chalice, and the manuscript, we are at a dead end. I will scan and email a copy of the manuscript and photos of the carvings on the three relics as well as the wooden cylinder and send it all out in advance, so they can get working.'

'So, in the meantime, what do we do?' Quinn asked.

Juliette spun around in her chair and waved at the skyline. 'Who needs to ask that when they are in Paris with forty-eight hours to kill?'

20

After a sleepless night and the following day spent mostly worrying about Jodie, Amy slipped her arm through Hunter's as they strolled along the Left Bank and watched the colours of Notre Dame cathedral's twin bell towers turn orange in the setting sun. The Seine sparkled in the same crisp, dying light, and all around, people were slowly enjoying the evening, despite the cold weather. With Jodie being held hostage by the mysterious new group, relaxing was impossible, but at least she knew her old friend and protégé was alive. She also had faith they would rescue her and bring her home safely.

They sat in a café and drank beer, watching the world go by, waiting anxiously for Juliette to call with news of the new expert. Blanco, Lewis, and Quinn had gone off somewhere else. Neither were sure where, or even if they were together.

'I think I need another beer,' Amy admitted after setting down her empty bottle. 'Call me pathetic, but it seems to help me cope with Jodie's kidnapping.'

Hunter ordered two more beers. 'I feel the same way, but I know she's going to be fine.'

'You think?' she asked. 'This isn't just what Juliette called your mindless optimism?'

'Not at all. You just have to think about it. Whoever has Jodie isn't going to harm her while they're waiting for us to deliver on the trade. After that, they might be planning on letting her go, or they might be planning on killing her.'

Amy winced.

'Sorry,' Hunter said, pausing for a sip of the beer. 'I'm just trying to say that right now she's safe, and as we're presuming they're going to try and kill not just her but all of us after the trade, we can plan for it in advance and make sure it doesn't happen. She's going to be fine. Trust me, I'm a doctor.'

'Yeah, of archaeology.'

'But this is an archaeological matter.'

She smiled. 'You're one of a kind, Max Hunter.'

'That's what my identical twin always says.'

'Wait a minute, you have an identical... Damn it.'

He laughed. 'Cannot believe you fell for that.'

After a pause, Amy said, 'You think we'll ever work out what de Gama has kept hidden for the past five hundred years?'

'I'm confident of it. We're the best at what we do, and so far we've already secured three of the five relics.'

'Aren't you forgetting the fifth one is almost certainly on the *Titanic*?'

'I am not forgetting that,' he said, smirking.

Amy lowered her beer bottle and narrowed her eyes at him. 'What are you up to, Max?'

He shrugged. 'Stuff.'

'What kind of stuff.'

'All right, call me crazy, but here's what I've been putting together. You remember Oskar Rorschach?'

'I'm hardly likely to forget him, Max. He's the only eccentric Swiss billionaire I ever met, his house was like Grand Central Station and he has a personal submarine yacht that... Oh no, you can't be serious.'

Hunter was so excited he could barely contain himself. 'I see you already put two and two together and made four.'

'You cannot be serious. You want to call up Oskar Rorschach and use his submarine yacht to dive down to the wreck of the *Titanic*?'

'Sure, and why not? If the idol really does turn out to be down there, then how else are we going to dive all the way to the wreck and look for it?

How many other people do you know with their own personal submarine? Any other way would take months to organise – longer considering it's a UNESCO site. The paperwork will be horrendous.'

'Hang on, aren't you supposed to be the guy arguing in favour of this paperwork keeping the site safe?'

'Under normal circumstances, yes. But these are not normal circumstances. Francisco de Gama was obviously hiding something of world-shattering importance for men like Bauer, and whoever this other lot who snatched Jodie is, to be carrying on like they are. It's just a hunch, but I think this could be the greatest find of our career.'

'Our very short career, and it has to top Atlantis, too. I'm not optimistic.'

'Open your mind! De Gama found something big, Amy. Big and important and maybe dangerous. We have a duty to find it too. We can only do that if we beat Bauer and these other maniacs down to the wreck and salvage the idol first.'

'You are insane.'

'No, but I do have an insane thirst for knowledge.'

When Juliette called Max's phone, they almost ran back to her office at UNESCO headquarters. Blanco, Lewis, and Quinn were already there, sitting around a large conference table in the office next to Juliette's. Professor Bonnaire herself brushed past them in the corridor, a thick wad of papers under her arm.

'You got here quick,' she said with a smile.

'We have no time to waste,' said Amy.

They followed her into the office and took a seat. Then a tall, slim woman with long blonde hair and fashionable tortoiseshell glasses walked into the room with an iPad under her arm. She was wearing a smart black business suit and when she shook Juliette's hand, she turned and gave Hunter a long, withering glance.

'Team HARPA,' Juliette said brightly. 'I'd like to introduce you to Professor Hanna Vikander from Stockholm University. She also works for us here at UNESCO. Perhaps Max here might have already told you about her.'

When Hunter saw Hanna's face, he sank into his chair, muttered something under his breath, closed his eyes, and gave a long, weary sigh. In

Amy's opinion, it looked a little like he might be hoping to find a hole to crawl into.

Hanna placed her iPad down on the table and frowned. 'Good evening, Maximillian.'

'Hello, Hanna,' Hunter said, opening his eyes and fixing them on her chilly gaze. 'I do hope life is treating you well.'

'Since you walked out on me, yes. Much better, thank you.'

Amy turned and glared at Hunter.

Along with everyone else in the room.

21

Amy Fox didn't know exactly what it was, but she knew Hunter's relationship with the Swedish semiotician must have been more than professional in the past. She guessed it must have also been more cordial in the past because right now the atmosphere between them was so cold it was like an iceberg had floated into the room.

'You two know each other, I take it?' Amy asked.

Hunter opened his mouth to speak, but Hanna cut him off.

'I think "knew" each other is a better way of putting it.'

'It was a long time ago,' Hunter said, satisfied that closed the matter.

'Not that long ago,' Hanna corrected him.

Hunter shrank further into his seat. 'No, perhaps not that long ago.'

Amy's frown deepened. 'You walked out on her?'

Hunter was wincing. 'I can actually feel the italics in that sentence, Amy. Weaponised italics.'

'Don't try to be funny,' she said. 'Because you're not funny. Not right now. And don't try to throw me off the scent.'

'I'm not trying to throw you off any scent. And I did not walk out on her.'

'It's Hanna,' Hanna said. 'Not her. And I'm standing right here, by the way.'

Hunter raised his palms in apology. 'You're quite right, that was rude and I apologise. I'll use your name from now on.' He turned back to Amy. 'Professor Vikander and I had a slight disagreement about the nature of our relationship and I decided to take some time out to reflect on it.'

The Swede sighed. 'What a long way around saying "walked out", Maximillian.'

'And would you stop calling me that? No has called me that since I was about twelve.'

'No, I don't think I will stop,' Hanna said with a smirk. 'I like calling you that.'

'Excellent,' Juliette said with a loud, forced laugh, clapping her hands together to draw a line under the conversation and move on. 'I can see we're going to have so much fun working together on this mission. I just know it.'

'Wait a minute!' Hunter and Hanna said at the exact same time.

'This is not a UNESCO mission,' Hunter said. 'Tell her, Amy. Do that thing where you get all American and FBI and lay the law down. You're good at that. No one messes with that.'

Amy gave him a look, one arched eyebrow and the ghost of a cynical smile. 'Thanks for that, Max, but the truth is we need Professor Vikander. You've already said you can't translate the symbols on these objects and Professor Bonnaire has been very clear that Professor Vikander is the best shot we have. I think you just have to suck this up.'

'Suck it up?' he said. 'Is that your professional advice?'

'It's not really advice when it's your boss saying it, Max,' Amy said with a sly wink.

Juliette laughed again. 'Wonderful, but let us move on. We have so little time and I'm afraid to say we also have much work to do. First, I need hardly tell you, Max, that the *Titanic* is a UNESCO-listed site, and as this mission seems to have something to do with the ship, I feel I have to make the case that we must be involved, at the very least in an oversight capacity. Second, we are behind the enemy, as you might say. And I was distressed to learn that Brodie McCabe has crawled out of the woodwork once again, and even more alarmed with the news he was still working for the Creed. Learning that Hans Bauer is this Magus character who Karl Adler was working for in the search for Atlantis has been both useful and shocking.'

Lewis nodded. 'Tell me about it. After Greenland, I was kind of hoping we'd seen the last of those guys forever, but apparently not.'

Juliette resumed control. 'Quite so. I have gathered everyone here tonight because Professor Vikander has news for us. As you all know, I asked her to look over the manuscript you found in Bauer's castle, as well as the strange carvings on the relics and the wooden cylinder.' She turned to Hanna and with a polite nod of the head, gestured for her to take over. 'Please, Professor Vikander, tell us what you know.'

Hanna stood to her full height of just under six feet and opened her folder to read some of her notes. She paused, probably for effect, Hunter thought cynically, and then raised her head to take in the expectant people staring up at her.

'I hope you know something we don't,' Hunter said. 'Because a woman's life depends on it. A woman we all care very much about.'

'Then it is a good thing I know where de Gama's crucifix is,' Hanna said.

A stunned silence fell over the group. 'Wait,' Amy said, turning to Hanna. 'What did you just say? You already know where it is?'

'I think so, yes. It might have fooled Max Hunter, but the clues from Bauer's castle were not so hard to untangle after all.'

Hunter crossed his arms and closed his eyes. Sinking into his seat, he said, 'Mea culpa, mea maxima culpa.'

'Naturally,' Hanna said.

'All right, so you worked it out,' Hunter said. 'Let's hear it then.'

'All in good time,' she said. 'First, I want to talk about Francisco De Gama, for context.'

Hunter stifled a yawn. 'Here we go. Context.'

Juliette glowered at Hunter. 'Please, Professor Vikander. Proceed.'

'Thank you. I have been doing a lot of research on this on the plane from Cambodia, and he's a very interesting character. Francisco de Gama was an explorer and a very brave man. He was also well-known for his love of puzzles and riddles. Apparently, it's always been speculated that he found somewhere or something of great historical importance on his adventures in the South American jungles, but exactly where or what was never known, until now.'

'But do we know where he ended up?' Juliette said.

'Not really. De Gama definitely returned from the New World,' Hanna said. 'We have a record of his journey on board a ship which set sail from Barranquilla in the late 1530s. Thanks to the treasures he found in the Americas, he was one of the wealthiest men in Spain upon his return, but his new life was not a happy one. I said earlier he was an explorer, but he was more than that. Francisco de Gama was a member of a group called the Alumbrados, a fifteenth-century Illuminati sect whose members were mercilessly persecuted by the Spanish Inquisition.'

'I bet they weren't expecting that,' Hunter said with a grin.

Amy closed her eyes and cricked her neck, sighing. 'Someone had to say it, I guess.'

'Say what?' asked Quinn.

'It's an old Monty Python joke from the third quarter of the last century,' Amy said with a frown.

'Ah, Hunter's era,' said Quinn.

'I am not that old,' said the archaeologist. 'Almost, but not quite.'

'If I can just steer this back to the business at hand,' Hanna said. 'De Gama was made aware by a colleague in the church that the Inquisition was coming for him. You see, his membership in the Alumbrados led to brutal persecution by the Catholic Church. All kinds of people were persecuted at that time right across Europe, and for any number of crimes against the Church.'

'And what was De Gama's crime?' said Blanco.

'Primarily, his membership of the Alumbrados,' Hanna said. 'It was a word the Inquisition used to describe a number of devout worshippers who created a new mystical cult in western Spain. The name Alumbrados derives from the Spanish verb to light up.'

'In other words,' Amy said, 'these men and women were illuminated?'

Hanna's smile faded. 'Yes.'

'In other words, you mean Illuminati,' Hunter said to a stunned room. 'Am I right?'

22

'You said that, not me,' Hanna said.

Juliette saw how unsettled the group had become and calmed everyone down. 'I know what you are all thinking, but just because de Gama was in a Spanish group called the Illuminated Ones, or whatever Alumbrados means precisely, does not mean the Illuminati are back on the scene today, and it does not, I repeat not, mean that is who took Jodie.'

'You're right,' Hunter said. 'Except it was obviously the Illuminati who snatched Jodie. Damn it, why didn't I work that out before?'

Juliette frowned. 'That is literally the opposite of what I just said, Max.'

'But think about it,' he continued. 'Remember what Adler told us when we were searching for Atlantis? About how the Illuminati no longer existed because it had turned into the Creed so long ago? Remember how he said that the Creed was a global group, but split into many different factions, some warring? What if one of those factions has decided to revert to the old ways and revive the Illuminati? Who else would know about what the Creed is looking for with de Gama's relics? It has to be them.'

'More from the Professor of Jumping to Conclusions a little later,' Hanna said. 'But right now, I am only halfway through my presentation.'

Hunter raised a palm. 'Sorry, please go ahead, Professor Vikander.'

'I will, thank you, Maximillian. Moving on to the strange wooden cylinder you found in the castle. This is called a scytale.'

'What's the sky got to do with anything?' Quinn asked.

Hanna spelled it out. 'The scytale is a cylindrical device used since ancient times as what we call a transitional cipher. In this case, the information in it was written in ancient Greek, but backward and legible only in a mirror. Then, it requires the scytale to decipher it, by winding the message around it. It's clear from not only the age and handwriting style but also the message context that it was written by de Gama himself.'

'But what does it say?' Quinn asked.

'It says he must flee Spain to escape persecution by the Inquisition. It says he has hidden five sacred relics in different locations. A ring in a church in Rome. A compass in a mansion owned by friends in Seville. A chalice in another church in Bohemia. An idol in Rouen cathedral and a crucifix in Barcelona cathedral.'

'Whoa!' Amy said, beaming at her team. 'We did it! The crucifix is in Barcelona. We know where the final relic is! We can trade them and save Jodie's life. Thank God.'

Everyone cheered except Hunter. He hadn't taken his eyes off Hanna Vikander and was worried by the look on her face.

Juliette saw it, too. 'You seem concerned by something, Professor Vikander.'

Hanna's eyes narrowed as she frowned and stared down at her translation of the scytale. She took a long breath. 'De Gama also says that whoever deciphers the secret message of the five sacred relics will find the Golden One.'

'El Dorado,' Hunter said, snapping his fingers. 'Gotta be. Colombia. Think about it.'

Hanna wasn't so sure. 'Maybe, maybe not. He also says the Golden One is not what any treasure hunter might think it is, and that any hunter should give up the search now, while he still can. I don't like it. This isn't a treasure map leading to riches, whether archaeological or gold. It's a warning telling people to stay away for their own good.'

'He's obviously just writing about a city of gold,' Hunter said cockily. 'And wants everyone else to stay away.'

'In which case, why leave clues on how to find it?' Amy asked.

Hunter paused a beat. 'I was waiting to see who would be the first to see that obvious point, and I'm not surprised to see it was Agent Fox. Well done, Amy.'

'Quit while you're still behind, Max,' Blanco said. 'Trust me. It's better this way.'

Hunter smiled. 'I still say it's El Dorado. But what exactly does he say about it, Professor Vikander?'

Hanna put on her reading glasses and looked down at her translation of the manuscript. 'He says, and I quote, "It was here that we found El Dorado, the Golden One. I was astonished, as were the rest of my party. We had heard rumours from other Europeans in the area, and legends spoken by local tribes, but presumed them all to be nothing more than deluded dreams and nonsense. When I crested that final rise in the jungle and saw the city walls, my breath was taken away fully from my body, and for a moment I thought my heart had stopped beating. We had found what locals spoke of in hushed, respectful whispers – an ancient city lost for millennia. Not even the Muisca had seen its deepest interior, its beating heart. Its provenance must surely be unknowable if that great and ancient tribe does not know it."'

'Holy moly,' Lewis said. 'I think Max is right. Sounds like he hit the jackpot. He found the ancient, lost city made entirely of gold.'

'Imagine its value today,' said Quinn, her eyes sparkling as she tried to do the math.

'No,' Hanna said, scanning the crumbling document. 'Please, listen to me. He doesn't ever describe the city as made of gold, not at all. All references to the city are simply "the lost city" or "the walled city" only, and nothing else. When he refers to El Dorado, he seems to be talking about something else.'

'How so?' Amy asked.

'Which is also my question,' Hunter said. 'How so?'

'It's hard to say,' continued Hanna, 'because he mentions that specific phrase so rarely, but when he talks about El Dorado, it seems more abstract, and also it's as if it's something inside the city, not the city itself. Most interesting, at the end, he clearly writes that it's not what he thought it would be.'

'What does he say, exactly?' Hunter asked. 'The archaeologist in me is officially enthralled.'

Hanna thumbed through the pages until she reached the end. 'Ah, yes. Here it is. I quote again. "Whoever named El Dorado the Golden One was understating what they had found, for it is quite simply the most awesome, terrifying, and wondrous thing any man can comprehend. Nestled deep in the heart of the lost city, El Dorado wields a power that dwarfs that of the most mighty of empires. A power that even now, merely contemplating it, has left my hands trembling."'

'And his writing is wobbly here, as he says,' Hanna said.

'What the hell does any of that mean?' asked Quinn.

Blanco shrugged. 'Could be anything, being honest.'

'The truth shall set you free, right?' Quinn said. 'If only we knew it.'

'De Gama knew it,' Hunter said. 'And I'm going to know it, too.'

'You mean *we're* going to know it,' said Amy.

'Yeah, sure. That's what I just said.'

Juliette stood up and rapped her knuckles on the desk. 'Then, there we have it. We know the crucifix is in Barcelona cathedral, and we know de Gama used his five sacred relics to lead treasure hunters to a clue to something he called the Golden One. You will need all five of these relics to know the precise location of this Golden One. We also know that the Creed and another association are presumably engaged in the search for this Golden One. Both groups have murdered for it and now one of them has kidnapped one of our own for it. They clearly mean business, but whether or not the second group is some kind of rival organisation to the Creed remains to be seen.'

'Illuminati,' Hunter said. 'Mark my words.'

'We know nothing of the sort,' Amy said. 'I think we should stay focused and professional and leave the speculation out.'

'Agreed,' Juliette said. 'And now you must get to work. I recommend you join the HARPA team on a temporary basis, Professor Vikander. Your unique skills may very well be required once again out in the field. Are you happy to join them?'

'Of course.'

'Are you happy to have the professor in your team, Agent Fox?'

'I think so, but I'll need to run it past Director Gates.'

'*Naturellement*,' Juliette said.

'You and me working together after all these years, Maximillian,' Hanna said with a thin smile. 'Won't that be fun?'

'If you say so,' he said, sinking even further into his chair.

'Don't be like that, Max,' Juliette said. 'I know you and Dr Vikander will be able to put your past behind you and work together like the professionals you both are to ensure this mission is brought to a successful close.'

'If you say so,' he said.

'Yes,' she said, glowering at him. 'I most certainly do say so, and I am your boss so I expect you to do it.'

'Wait a minute,' Amy said. 'I'm his boss!'

Juliette shrugged and muttered in French.

'Hardly matters though,' Amy said with a wicked grin.

'Why not?' Max asked.

'Because I also expect you and Dr Vikander to put your past behind you and work together like the professionals you both are to ensure this mission is brought to a successful close.'

Juliette laughed. 'There, you see? You have nowhere to run. Poor little Max.'

* * *

Olav Skulberg had been waiting patiently for the call. When Jørgen Dahl walked over to him with a phone in his hand, he almost snatched it away from him. Lifting it to his face, he lowered his voice and spoke into the speaker.

'Coelho, I understand you have some news for me on Njord.'

'Yes, Admiral. It's looking like our launch window is narrowing. We need to expedite the programme by several days.'

Skulberg was afraid of this. 'Is that possible?'

'Yes, I can do it just as soon as you give the order. If we're not careful and we don't move fast, we could lose everything we have all worked for across the years. It would be a catastrophe.'

'Then you have your orders. Expedite Njord. But only if everything can be executed safely. I don't want to lose any more men on this mission.'

'I understand.'

'We have waited a long time for this, Coelho. A very long time. The treasure is in our grasp, closer than ever before. I cannot and will not allow anything or anyone to get in the way. That is why you have my permission to do whatever it takes to ensure the success of Operation Njord. Is that clear?'

The Portuguese man confirmed that he understood, and Skulberg ended the call, handing the phone back to Dahl. Outside the window of his snug, the mists were thicker than ever, but his trusty fire kept him warm. He reached for the glass of single malt on his mantelpiece and took a long, slow sip. Felt it burning its way down inside him. A smile flickered on his lips and then his lined, wrinkled face was suddenly all business again.

'Things are moving faster than we expected, Jørgen. If we don't act now, we could lose everything we have striven for. Everything is in jeopardy, old friend. Njord hangs by a thread.'

'Is Coelho moving on with the plans now?'

Skulberg nodded. 'Yes, and let us pray it's not too late.'

23

Team HARPA landed at El-Prat Airport out on the coast to the south of Barcelona. After a few quick moments being rushed through customs thanks to some advance words by Jim Gates and Juliette Bonnaire, they found themselves outside in the parking lot climbing into a large, brand-new SUV. The day was warm compared with Austria, with a clear blue sky and a bright, mild sun.

The districts flashed by in a blur. L'Hospitalet de Llobregat, La Bordeta, Sant Antoni. With over one and a half million residents, the only bigger city in Spain was Madrid; this was clear as Blanco whisked them deep into its ancient heart in a hired Hilux. The quiet Brooklynite said nothing as he drove, keeping his eyes either fixed on the road or scanning the mirrors for any unwanted followers. Deftly sweeping across junctions and weaving in and out of city buses and cabs, he drew the team ever closer to their destination. He turned right and cruised through El Raval before driving into a winding labyrinth of narrow side streets lined with terracotta-roofed townhouses.

'So, what exactly is the story between you and the good Dr Vikander?' Amy whispered into Hunter's ear. They were sitting in the back seat of the Hilux, just behind Lewis and Quinn, who were sitting in the middle seats. Up front, Hanna was keeping Blanco company.

'Story? There's no story.'

'Pull the other one, Max.'

'What do you mean?' he asked innocently.

She sighed. 'Nothing at all.'

'There's no story! I remember hardly anything about that summer.'

'Charming,' she said, peering forward to the windshield. Up ahead of them, Barcelona cathedral came into view. 'Heads up.'

'Yup, we're here,' Blanco said, turning slightly in his seat. 'I'm going to pull in just up here on the side of the road.'

'Looks pretty busy,' Hanna said. 'Lots of tourists.'

'It's a beautiful cathedral and a beautiful day,' Lewis said. 'Bound to be lots of tourists here taking pictures and catching a few rays.'

Blanco slowed the car and parked in a long line of cars on Carrer de Ferran, at the northern end near the Plaça de Sant Jaume, a nineteenth-century square nestled in the Old City that had once been the centre of the ancient Roman settlement here. They stepped out of the Hilux into the afternoon and slipped on baseball hats and shades, just in case anyone unpleasant might have hacked into the city's CCTV system. Hunter was not a fan of the cloak and dagger routine but understood why it was necessary and put on his hat and glasses just like the rest of the team.

Amy gave him a look. 'It's for our own protection, Max.'

'If it makes you happy, Amy,' he said with a smile, 'I'll do anything. Maybe we should stand outside the basilica and have a long kiss to just complete the image of us being harmless tourists.'

'Maybe later,' she said as she adjusted her hat. 'If you're a good boy.'

'I'm always good, but more often bloody brilliant.'

Hanna shook her head in despair but was unable to hide her smile. 'Is there no off-switch on you, Hunter?'

'Maybe,' he said. 'You can try to find it if you like – but only if your hands are warm.'

Hanna's smile faded. 'Ugh. I've already been there and it's a no from me.'

Amy looked at him. 'Yeah, that's not being a good boy. Request for kiss denied.'

Blanco laughed. 'You blew that one, soldier.'

'Yeah, I think I might have.'

They crossed the square and walked along more side streets, passing smiling pedestrians and busy little shops. The occasional Vespa buzzed by. In ever-narrowing walkways, the buildings loomed high above them and blocked the sun. Lewis and Quinn were up ahead of them and suddenly pulled up to a stop in the alleyway. When Hunter and the others joined them, they knew why. Looming above them was the massive thirteenth-century cathedral stretching high into the blue sky, its intricate Gothic architecture reflecting the bright sunshine.

'Ladies and gentlemen,' said Lewis. 'I give you the Cathedral of the Holy Cross and Saint Eulalia, otherwise known as Barcelona Cathedral.'

'Whoa,' Hanna said. 'Big.'

'And beautiful,' said Amy. 'When was this built?'

'Serious work began on the first of May 1298,' Lewis said, admiring the ancient Gothic architecture. 'And finally ended in 1448. That's a hundred and fifty years.'

'A hundred and fifty years?' Hanna said, breaking away from the group. 'That's a long time.'

'Nearly as long as it's going to take to design a working one-way traffic system in Oxford,' Hunter said. 'So many happy memories of that place, it's hard to know which one to repress first.'

'There can't be much room left in there after repressing so many Hanna Vikander memories,' Amy said with a smirk.

'Talking of whom,' Quinn said. 'I spy Dr Vikander making her way over to the cathedral steps.'

'Always running ahead of time,' Hunter said. 'Nothing changes.'

'Oh my, doesn't she look grand in that wonderful straw sunhat,' Amy said.

Hunter fixed her with one of his glances. 'Let's not get personal. She has a very low tolerance for the sunshine.'

'Or arrogant men, by the sound of it,' Quinn said.

'Ouch,' said Lewis.

Hunter stepped out behind Hanna and turned to peer back at his friends. 'Shall we get on?'

Amy was first to follow Hunter. She looked up and down the narrow road lined with sycamore trees and small businesses. The sun beat down through the leaves, producing mottled shadows that flicked over them as they walked along.

'That's not what I was expecting,' Quinn said, looking at the cathedral.

'What were you expecting?' Amy asked.

'I don't know, but not that.'

Lewis worked it out first. 'Ah, I think you were thinking about the world-famous Basilica de la Sagrada Família. The late 1800s through to the early 1900s. Designed by the famous architect Antoni Gaudí. Still unfinished – somewhat famously so.'

'It's a UNESCO World Heritage Site,' Hunter said. 'Naturally.'

'Is there anywhere that is not a UNESCO World Heritage Site?' Quinn asked.

'I doubt your hometown is,' Hunter said. 'And where is that, by the way?'

After raising her middle finger at him, she turned and walked away from him, pulling out her phone and snapping a few pictures of the much older Catholic cathedral ahead of them. Seeing them approach, Hanna Vikander saw them and gave them a cheery wave. She had raced ahead and was now standing at the bottom of the cathedral's steps, her sky-blue summer dress and sun-bleached straw hat bright in the sun. As Hunter drew closer, he found it hard to take his eyes off her.

'Memories coming back now, soldier?' Amy asked, noticing.

'Eh? Oh yeah... I mean, no.'

'Only, you seem to be staring at Dr Vikander.'

'Nonsense,' he said, moving his gaze up to the cathedral. 'I was simply admiring the flying buttresses.'

She shook her head and ignored him, taking the lead and walking over to the Swede. 'You really streaked ahead of us there, Dr Vikander.'

'I'm keen to get on, that is all,' she said tartly.

They walked inside, passing through security among a large crowd of tourists, and after asking at an information desk for their contact, were told to wait to one side. Moments later, a man in a black cassock seemed to float across the flagstones, smiling as he neared them.

'*Buenos días,*' he said, offering a warm handshake. 'I am Monsignor Pedro Pérez, the Dean of the Cathedral of the Holy Cross and Saint Eulalia. Welcome.'

'It's nice to meet you, *monsignor*,' Amy said, returning the handshake and introducing the team. 'It's very good of you to allow us access to your vaults at such short notice.'

He waved it away. '*De nada*. The archbishop asked me personally to assist you in your investigation,' he said, smiling. 'It's not every day we have the opportunity to help law enforcement, and you being part of both the FBI and UNESCO caused quite a stir in the offices this morning when we found out you were coming.'

'I hope we're not inconveniencing the cathedral too much.'

'Not at all. If you please follow me, I've already arranged for you to visit the vault where we keep some of our holiest relics and other rare pieces.' After a long stroll through the cathedral, they reached a thick wooden door. When Pérez opened it, it gave a hoarse, pained groan which echoed all around them. He turned and smiled. 'What you seek is just through here.'

They walked down some stone steps until another thick wooden door blocked their path. Pérez worked his way through the thick iron keys, mumbling to himself. Then, he inserted the chosen key in the lock and opened the final door, leading them into a small, stone room filled with old chests.

'At last! What you are seeking is here,' he said, wandering over to one of the chests. He stopped and turned. 'No, here, in this one.'

Amy glanced at her watch and looked sidelong at Hunter. 'We don't have much time.'

Pérez wasn't listening. He was rummaging around inside one of the chests. When he produced something wrapped in an old linen cloth, Amy almost gasped.

'If I am not very much mistaken, this is what you desire.' Pérez unwrapped a beautiful, ornate golden crucifix covered in sparkling jewels of every kind. Diamonds, sapphires, emeralds, rubies.

'Thank you!' Amy said. 'I think this must surely be it.'

Pérez grew sombre. 'Now, this is the property of the cathedral. I have already spoken with Professor Bonnaire at UNESCO and we have agreed to lend it to you for a limited time in order to get your friend back and complete your mission. After this, you must return it to us. These are the conditions of use.'

'Of course,' Hunter said, taking hold of the relic. 'It's a marvel.'

They moved back upstairs and found themselves once again in the warm, sunlit nave.

'This is most helpful of you,' Amy said. 'Thank you on behalf of the United States government.'

'And you are most welcome.' Pérez locked the door to the vault. 'Do you have a secure mode of transport for the crucifix?'

'Certainly. It'll be safe with us.'

'It really is a beautiful relic,' Hunter said, admiring it.

'It certainly is.' Hanna Vikander took the crucifix from Hunter and stepped into the light of some sunrays spilling down through a giant stained-glass window above them. 'Now, I need to examine this artifact in silence and compare the inscription to that on the other relics.'

The team gave her some space and broke apart to wander around the cathedral and take in the impressive medieval architecture. Hunter had made only a few steps when a deep explosion emanated from the other end of the vast cathedral.

'Bloody hell!' he said. 'That sounded like a grenade!'

Hanna turned and stared at him, horrified. 'A grenade? You can't be serious!'

A second explosion rocked the cathedral, the sound of the detonation echoing down the massive central nave and forcing some masonry to break away from the top of the arcades and smash down onto the tiled floor.

Tourists screamed and ran in all directions.

'Yeah,' Hunter said. 'Pretty serious.'

Pérez made the sign of the cross over his face and chest. 'What is this about?'

'It's about some very unpleasant men trying to steal de Gama's crucifix,' Amy said, almost apologetically. 'I'm sorry.'

'What?' he asked. 'You never told me your presence here would put the cathedral or any of the staff in danger!'

'We had no idea they knew about the crucifix being here, *monsignor!*' Amy said defensively.

At her side, Lewis peeled away and ran towards the noise. All around, the chatter of submachineguns tore through the silence of the nave, making everyone jump.

'This is an abomination!' Pérez said. 'Who are these people? And how dare they enter the House of God with these appalling weapons and threaten people!'

Another peel of gunshots, a deep metallic roar as rounds sprayed all over the place. This time, they were followed by the sound of people screaming. Terrible, mangled cries scratching off the walls and roof high above them. Hunter had heard those sorts of sounds before, in heavy combat.

'I think they're doing more than threatening people,' Hunter said.

'Holy crap!' cried Lewis, returning from the other end of the nave. 'They're killing anyone who gets in their way.'

'I'm guessing they already killed the security, too?' Blanco said.

Hanna nodded. 'First thing they did.'

'But who are these monsters?' Pérez asked for the second time.

'Monsters is the right word,' Quinn replied. 'Call me paranoid,' she said, 'but something tells me those guys aren't here to pray to God.'

When the men burst inside their part of the nave, they immediately opened fire, spraying rounds all over the place and making the remaining tourists, worshippers, and staff scatter for their lives like terrified sheep.

The half-dozen men in the central aisle were walking faster now, arms reaching into their black leather jackets for concealed weapons. The man in the lead pulled his gun to reveal it was fitted with a suppressor. When he turned and fired three shots into the security guard's chest, blasting him against the stone pillar and killing him instantly, their intention was clear.

Quinn gasped and took a step back in horror. 'How did they get here so fast?'

'That doesn't matter,' Amy said. 'All that matters now is that we get the hell away from them, and right now! Take cover!' she yelled.

The team dashed behind several large pillars stretching up to the roof, but for Pérez, who was already halfway down the main aisle when the attack happened, it was too late. One of the men turned his submachinegun on him and ripped him to shreds. The rounds tore through him and continued on their way, blasting chunks out of the wooden pews beside him. The old man collapsed to the floor in a bloody heap, his lips uttering a final prayer to God before his life slipped away.

'We're out of here,' Amy said. 'Side door, twenty yards to our left. Right now.'

24

Outside, just behind where their car was parked, they saw two black Jeep Cherokees, their paintwork reflecting the bright Spanish sun in a dazzling flash. Inside, they could just make out a number of men wearing sunglasses but they were mostly obscured by the shade inside the vehicles.

'I knew they'd find us,' Amy said. 'But not this fast. These guys are really good.'

'But who are they?' Quinn asked. 'Creed or Illuminati?'

'Creed,' Blanco said without hesitation. 'Illuminati are waiting for us to come to them, remember?'

'We can worry about how good they are later,' Hunter said. 'Right now, we need to be making some serious tracks.'

They jogged down the steps in front of the cathedral, Hunter leading the way with Amy beside him, then Quinn, Hanna, and Lewis in the middle and Blanco at the rear. They weaved quickly through more tourists on their way into the cathedral and then walked along the sidewalk back towards their cars. Hunter stepped out in front of a taxicab and held it up with his hand as he waved the rest of the team across the road.

'You're one hell of a crossing guard, Hunter,' Quinn said as she rushed past him.

'Thanks.'

Back at the top of the cathedral steps, the men who had murdered Pérez appeared in the large double doorway and waved over at the men in Jeeps parked further down the street. As the men on the steps renewed their attack, Hunter was already considering that they should have killed them back in the cathedral. Letting them live had only added to their mounting troubles.

'They're onto us again,' he said, turning and following the others onto the other side of the road.

'They've been onto us since the very beginning,' Lewis said. 'And Amy's right. They're really good.'

'Into the car,' Hunter said, turning to Blanco. 'Without Jodie, Sal's our next best driver, so you're at the wheel.'

Blanco said nothing. Having presumed this was going to happen, he was already climbing up into the driver's seat and sliding on his belt. Behind them, the men in black had exited the Jeep and were walking across the road towards the men who had just left the cathedral. They argued for a few seconds and then pointed over at their quarry.

Seeing the last of the HARPA team getting inside the SUV and slamming the door shut, the men now turned and ran back to their Jeeps. By the time Blanco had pulled out onto the road, the Jeep's engine was already running, the driver waiting for the last of his associates to get in. Seconds later, the engine revved and growled and the tyres squealed as they pulled out and drove up behind the SUV.

'Right on our ass,' Quinn said.

Hunter said, 'So, no dawdling please, Sal!'

As usual, Blanco had slipped into drive-mode and made no reply. Instead, he checked his mirror, increased speed, and began a series of dangerous but well-executed overtaking manoeuvres that started to put some space between them and their pursuers. After a few more of these, he spoke to anyone who was listening. 'Gonna need some directions, guys.'

'I'm on it,' Quinn said. 'Looks like you can go left up ahead. It's some kind of back street running behind the far side of the cathedral.'

A bullet pinged off the rear coachwork and ricocheted off into the sky. Everyone inside the car jumped. Lewis was in the back. He turned and saw one of the men leaning out of the front passenger's window of the Jeep directly behind, handgun aimed right at them. 'That escalated quickly.'

Amy said, 'You think we can lose them down that back street, Sal?'

'Won't know till I get down there.'

He hit the gas and forced his way around a small delivery van trundling along in front of them, then he spun the wheel hard to the left, mounted the curb, and swerved into the alley, giving their pursuers zero warning.

'They missed the turn,' Lewis said, pulling his gun out and checking the mag.

'Maybe they didn't see us come down here,' said Hanna. 'Just maybe, right?'

Amy's sigh of relief was cut short by Blanco's gravelly voice. 'Nope, they're reversing and heading right down here.'

'And they just hit a woman crossing the road,' Quinn said, leaning over the back seat beside Lewis and staring out through the rear window. 'These guys are real assholes.'

'Fifty yards and closing, Sal,' said Lewis.

Blanco raced the large SUV down the narrow cobblestone back street, carefully avoiding clipping the curbs as he planned his next move. The issue was not simply that they were zooming towards the end of the little street, but that there were a number of pedestrians passing back and forth up ahead.

'Left or right, Quinn?'

'Right.'

Blanco sounded the horn. The pedestrians turned and stared at the powerful SUV as it bore down on them, then scattered like sheep and cleared the way. He took immediate advantage, bursting out of the back street and spinning the wheel hard to the right. They almost tipped up onto two wheels as he smashed through a line of dumpsters, raced around the corner, and pulled onto a much busier road.

'Gross,' Quinn said, noting the garbage from the trash can smeared all over the windshield.

Blanco hit the wipers and cleared the filth away, leaving long trails of slime all over it. After a few washes from the jets, they were almost back to new. Then, a bullet from behind shattered the rear window.

'I guess we didn't lose them then,' said Hunter.

Blanco was weaving in and out of more traffic. 'More directions, please. Looks like we have a real problem coming up.'

25

Hunter peered through the SUV's windshield and saw two police cars forming a temporary roadblock directly ahead of them. One of the officers had drawn his sidearm and another was shepherding people away from the scene, quickly directing them inside shops and away from the road and sidewalks. 'That's not good.'

'Hardly surprising, what with the shooting and all,' said Lewis.

Quinn called out to Blanco. 'You can go left just before we get to the cops.'

'Done,' Blanco said. 'Thanks, Q.' He spun the wheel again and ploughed them around another corner, narrowly missing more pedestrians, who now waved their fists and screamed at them. 'I tried...' he said with a shrug.

'You definitely tried harder than the guys behind us,' Lewis said. 'They just ate up another pedestrian with the front of their Jeep.' The ex-US Marine was still looking out the back window, trying to make out some detail through the shattered glass. Twisting his neck around to face the others, he shook his head in disgust. 'That guy back there on the sidewalk was someone's son.'

'They're just bastards,' Quinn said. 'And it's the next right, Sal.'

'Got it. Thanks.'

Another bullet struck the back of the car with a deep metallic clunk.

Back where the man had fired the gun in the first Jeep, mayhem filled the air and pedestrians screamed all over again and ran for cover wherever they could find it.

Blanco felt the wheel slide through his hand as the wheels corrected back around to their normal direction. He checked the mirror. Hit the gas. Quietly enjoyed the thrill of the chase and the way the power of the engine pushed him back in his seat when he accelerated. Up ahead, the road looked clearer. This made him smile until he realized why. All lanes in both directions had been shut off by more police and a police helicopter was hovering over some high residential buildings off to their right.

'We need another road, Quinn. Cops shut this one down too.'

'Then it's the next left.'

'Damn it!' Hanna said. 'We need to get out of here. We're just going around in circles.'

'No, we're not,' said Blanco. 'We've been tracking north most of the time.'

Amy said, 'But now it's time to lose our friends, and I have an idea.'

'Then please enlighten us.'

'Look up ahead.'

'What am I looking at?' said Blanco, squinting through the sun's glare on the windshield. They were passing through the University Zone and heading into La Miranda.

'Looks like we can get up into the hills,' Amy said, 'and lose them there. We can't risk them getting any of the relics, Sal. They're our only way to buy Jodie's life.'

Blanco agreed and turned the car off the main road, driving away from the city and up into the hills to the city's northwest. In seconds, the urban sprawl had given way to dry dusty slopes covered in Aleppo pines and Judas trees.

'They're still behind us,' Lewis said.

'Damn it, coverage is out,' Quinn said, typing into her computer. 'We're driving blind, Sal. Sorry.'

Another round punched through the back tyre and sent the speeding SUV swerving wildly through a wooden five-bar gate and onto the side of an unsealed track, spitting up gravel chips and dust from the path in a swirling vortex behind them. Blanco steered into the skid and brought the car around in a perfect half-circle until they were facing the opposite direction. He slammed the brakes down and stopped the car dead. Dust from the path billowed up around them and blew through the open windows.

Quinn heard a woman screaming and peered through her window in time to see a young mother snatch up her child and run through some nearby bushes with her, heading back to a small, white-painted farmhouse. Maybe the farmer's wife and child, terrified, she thought. The sound of Lewis smacking another mag into his gun filled the car. Then the sound of sirens and a police chopper grew ever louder. The dust settled around them.

'Where are they?' Amy asked. 'Anyone see them? Did we lose them?'

Blanco was silent. They were all silent. The engine ticked over.

'You see them?' Hanna said, terrified.

Beside him, Quinn turned and looked back at the smashed gate. She saw the black Jeep rip past it just as they had done, and her heart sank. 'Still on our tail. Sorry.'

'We just can't shake these guys off,' Amy said. 'They're totally insane about getting the symbols on this crucifix.'

'And it's not hard to see why,' Hunter said. 'We don't know what de Gama found on his travels in the jungle, but if the crucifix helps you get there, then they need it just as badly as we do. And now it's time to end this.' He swung open the door and stepped out.

'Are you crazy?' Quinn called out.

Hunter raised his gun and walked around in front of their SUV, cool and calm. Then, standing in the middle of the track, he aimed at the first Jeep speeding towards them and fired half a dozen rounds into the front tyres. They ripped the rubber to shreds and the driver lost control. Hunter watched the Jeep tear off the track, smash through a wire fence and tip over down the slope, rolling all the way down and smashing into a tree at the bottom. It exploded in flames, the intense inferno consuming everyone inside before they even had a chance to unbuckle their belts.

Ahead, the second Jeep raced towards him. He raised his gun once again and this time fired into the windshield. The bullets found their mark and the driver was killed, sending the Jeep into a wild, hard turn to the right, away from the slope. The arc it was attempting was too sharp for the speed and now it tipped over, crashing onto the ground and skidding through the gravel with an ear-bending scraping of metal.

The men stumbled from the car and reached for their weapons. Using the upturned SUV as cover, they opened fire, not on HARPA but the police helicopter. After a sustained barrage, one of the shooters damaged the tail rotor. Hunter and the rest of the team watched in horror as the police chopper spun around helplessly before crashing down into the dry Spanish hillside and exploding into flames even wilder than the burning car wreck.

There was no time to react. The men now turned their fire on him. Hunter scrambled back to the relative safety of the SUV and joined in with his team, returning fire on the men behind the upturned Jeep, punching bullet holes in the windshield and pinging off the hoods and side panels. Blanco hit the man who had been driving and blood spouted from his neck as he slumped down in the dirt. Behind him, a third and fourth black Jeep swerved into view at the head of a column of dust.

Amy fired on a man at the rear of the upturned Jeep, filling him with holes and forcing the others around the back of the Jeep to find cover. Safe behind the Jeep, they now returned fire and perforated the SUV's roof with rounds. Lewis and Blanco broke free from the SUV and made it to the cover of a tree a few yards away. This gave them a better angle on the men behind the upturned Jeep, and now they opened fire, riddling another two of them with bullets and sending their jerking bodies down into the dust to die. Lewis fired on the gas tank and sent the vehicle rocketing into a third fierce explosion.

The others continued to fire on the remaining men. Hunter blew out the front tyres of the third Jeep and sent it into a wild, uncontrollable skid all over the road. It mounted a line of large stones at the side of the track with an axle-busting crunch and spun off into the dust. Swerving to a halt, the men inside kicked open the doors and staggered out, guns flashing in the sun.

The fourth Jeep skidded to a halt behind the carnage at the bottom of an embankment to their right. Back behind the SUV, Amy and Hunter and the others were unable to get a direct shot at most of the men, and worse, they could hear more police sirens approaching fast, this time on cars. They prayed the other side was just as keen to avoid local law enforcement as they were, and their prayers were answered. One of the men tapped his earpiece and cocked his head to hear better. He said a few words into his palm mic, grabbed his associate, and then the remaining men turned and fled down the embankment. Seconds later, the doors on the fourth black Jeep swung open. The men piled inside and then the Jeep sped away in a squeal of spinning tyres and burnt rubber.

'And we need to get out of here too,' Amy said. 'Fast.'

26

The mood was sombre as the team gathered their thoughts after the Creed's latest attempt to get their hands on the relics. The latest one they had secured, the crucifix, now sparkled in the dying sun falling through the window onto the bed.

Hanna Vikander gave a quiet sigh as she stared at it. 'I can't believe a man died today, over this. It's such an insane waste of life.' She grew quiet. 'I never saw anyone die before. And murdered as well. And those terrible explosions back upon the hill. Hideous.'

'I'm sorry,' Amy said. 'If we seem like we don't care, it's not that. We've all seen a lot of death and suffering in this team. Being used to it isn't the right way of putting it, but it's something we've all learned to live with.'

'Yeah, it's a real joy,' Quinn said.

The door swung open. Lewis was standing there smiling, his arms full of takeout bags.

Hanna nodded slowly, lost in contemplation of Amy's comforting words. After a long pause, she said, 'I wonder if old de Gama knew how much trouble he'd end up causing.'

'Probably,' Amy said, sipping some water and looking hungrily at the big plastic bag full of takeout cartons on the desk in front of her. 'But first, I want some of these tapas. It smells good and I'm famished. Who knew you could get this to go?'

Quinn was already opening up a carton of calamari and mushrooms. 'Looks okay. Rather have a burger.'

'Yeah, well,' Amy said with a sigh. 'This place was closer to the hotel. Sorry about that. You'll just have to suffer with this delicious array of Spanish tapas instead. Think about what Jodie is eating tonight.'

Quinn shrugged and picked at the mushrooms and finally ate some of the calamari. 'It's all right, I guess.'

'Talk about damning with faint praise,' said Hunter, sipping at his water.

'Get lost, Hunter.'

Hunter went to reply, but Amy stopped him. 'How about we all just sit here and eat and try to work out just what the hell we're going to do next.'

'Agreed,' Hunter said.

They were sitting around in a small hotel room they'd booked just outside the city's west. The land outside the window was dry and dusty. Olive-coloured trees and scrubby bushes partially covered a highway overpass, looming above the cheap hotel on chunky, graffitied concrete stanchions. A low sun, sinking down into the west, was throwing cool shadows from the busy road down over their window.

'One thing's for sure,' Quinn offered. 'The Creed is not going to stop coming after us. We have the crucifix and they do not. They haven't even seen it. They need it to complete de Gama's riddle and that means they need us, too.'

'Talking of which,' Lewis said, swallowing some beef and taking a refreshing sip of water. 'We need to get started on that riddle. Any grand epiphanies from our two experts, Max or Hanna?'

Hunter was also eating. Now, he smiled through a mouthful of the tapas and gestured for them to wait until he swallowed. 'I was wondering how long it would be until someone asked about my little epiphanies – and glorious they are, too. My last musings on the matter were enhanced, I thought, by the sunlight streaming in down through the stained-glass windows. I felt like I'd been touched by God himself.'

Hanna almost choked on her calamari. 'Damn it, Maximillian. Your arrogance nearly just killed me,' she said, coughing and reaching for some water.

'I was making le joke,' he said. 'No arrogance was even implied. Promise.'

She smiled.

Hunter saw the smile. 'This time, however, I must defer to my colleague, Dr Vikander. Her expertise in deciphering the symbols is second to none, after all.'

The Swede said, 'Sadly, I have not had enough time to properly translate the symbols on the crucifix. But thank you, Max.'

Quinn smirked. 'Wait, is the ice between you two finally thawing?'

'I think not,' Hanna said, looking back down at her meal.

The ensuing awkward silence was broken by Hunter's phone ringing. He didn't seem to hear it. He was still watching Hanna.

'Max,' Amy said. 'Max!'

'Oh, sorry.'

He left the room to take the call. When he returned, he was smiling. 'That was Juliette. She just got a call from the Illuminati – sorry, I mean Alumbrados. Apparently, they've already heard about our little adventure at the cathedral today, and our successful acquisition of the crucifix, so they're ready to trade. If we want to save Jodie's life, we have to go to Montserrat Cathedral just outside of Barcelona. Tonight. Eleven o'clock. No tricks or funny business, et cetera. You know the drill.'

The group shared a look, half confident, half anxious.

'Eat up, everyone,' Amy said. 'We have an old friend to go save.'

27

Monsignor Domingo Razquin, the abbot of Montserrat Monastery, was good at keeping secrets. More than that, he revelled in the quiet power his secrets endowed him with. His position at the world-famous monastery had been secured after the usual secret ballot, which in his case was entirely rigged by his Illuminati brethren. Easily done, especially among such trusting folk as here. Those who had not supported him or turned a blind eye had met their maker at the barrel of a gun.

This evening, he stood in his private offices at the very top of the monastery and considered the recent success of his forces across the continent in the Austrian castle. They had successfully raided the hated Creed's inner sanctum and burned it to the ground, just as they had promised would happen all those months ago. Further, they had secured a solid-gold bargaining chip in the form of Agent Jodie Priest. The young woman from HARPA would prove a valuable asset when it came to keeping the rest of her meddling team at bay during this critical time and forcing the delivery of de Gama's relics.

He turned to his loyal servant Belial, his voice low and weak. 'Bring me the girl.'

Sometime later, the giant Disciple dragged Jodie Priest into the room.

'What the hell do you want with me?' she said.

'Tell me what else you discovered at Bauer's castle beside the relics.'

'Get lost.'

'Was there a manuscript?'

'Go to hell.'

He laughed. 'We are already in hell, you and me. All of us.'

'I'll tell you nothing.'

He nodded. All to be expected. 'I know what you think you are seeking. You think you are seeking El Dorado,' Razquin said. 'But no one knows what is really in that notorious lost city. Not even the Creed. Only we, here, know what truly lies in the heart of that mountainous jungle, and it's not something anyone should be trifling with. Bring her closer!'

The giant Disciple Abaddon stepped forward. He grabbed Jodie's arm and wrenched her roughly over to where the ancient Illuminati master was standing. It was now she saw for the first time the old man's thin, withered face and dry, grey lips. He looked like he was about to drop down dead.

'Whatever you think I'm going to do for you,' she told him, 'you can forget it.'

He grinned and nodded. Old, yellow teeth, dry, dusty eyes. 'I like a young woman with proper fighting spirit. I read this about you some time ago, back when you were trampling all over the prettier parts of the world in pursuit of Atlantis. How did that dream end for you?'

'Get lost, psycho.'

He raised his hand and gently swept her hair from her face, then slapped her hard across her cheek before breaking into uncontrollable laughter. 'Psycho. I love this.'

When they knew it was safe to do so, Abaddon and the other Disciples in the room also began laughing cruelly.

'You will tell me what I want to know, Agent Priest,' said the abbot. 'And you will tell me now, or I will be forced to get the information out of you in very unpleasant ways. This is something I have done many times before. I can guarantee your compliance in the end. Speak now, and save this beautiful young face from eternal ruin. De Gama was once in our ranks, in the Alumbrados, but his treasures have been lost to us long ago. Hopefully, not for much longer. Now, was there a manuscript in the Creed's inner sanctum?'

'I told you, I will not cooperate.'

Razquin turned and walked away from her, stepping slowly over to the roaring fire. Built into an impressively large, gothic stone fireplace, it crackled and radiated a powerful heat into his private offices. He raised his hands and turned his palms to the flames.

'Ah, you are too young to know how good it feels to warm such old bones.' He laughed. '"Now the king was sitting in the winter house in the ninth month, with a burning fire in the brazier before him."'

Jodie looked confused. 'Huh?'

'Jeremiah 36:22,' the abbot said coldly. 'It's a verse in their favourite book.'

'Their book?'

'Christians,' he said flatly. 'Now, Belial, please fetch the irons. Time is short and we have much to do. We need to know what this woman knows and we need to know it now.'

'Yes, Master,' Belial said, padding over to a small wooden door beside the fireplace. He opened the door with a black iron key and swung it open with an ear-piercing scratching sound. After a few moments rummaging around inside the room, he stepped back into the light, cobwebs lightly covering his shoulders and hair. He was holding three fire irons.

Branding irons.

Razquin slipped the hood from his cloak over his head, looked at the irons, and then at Jodie. Returning his gaze to the irons in Belial's hands, he said slowly, 'Eeny, meeny, miny, moe...'

'What the hell is this?' Jodie said, kicking and squirming in Abaddon's giant grip. 'You people are insane.' She felt sick with fear but was determined not to show it, not to give these men any satisfaction or encouragement. Still, the thought of being back with her friends, joking around with Hunter or enjoying a quiet smoke with Blanco, and then waking from the daydream to see these evil maniacs around her, made her want to break down and cry.

'These are branding irons,' Razquin said. 'They're for branding wood and leather, but I had these specially designed with my personal emblems on them. This one has my initials. This one has my coat of arms, and this one is the sign of the Illuminati. Which one would you like permanently burned into your face?'

Jodie kicked more, but it was useless. When Belial passed the irons to the master, he took hold of some rope and tied her legs together while she was still in Abaddon's grip. The master chuckled and walked over to the fire, gently pushing the irons into the burning embers to heat them. She watched the back of his head, now hidden inside the black hood. It swayed gently from side to side as he sang a perverse, unsettling tune in Latin. She heard a scraping noise as he pulled one of the irons out of the logs and then he turned, a terrible, grisly smile on his face.

'I am looking forward to this so much, I almost want you to hold your tongue.'

'Please,' she cried out. 'I don't know what you want me to say. Please, don't put that thing on my face!'

'Then you must tell me what your team has found out about de Gama's expedition into the jungle. You must tell me if there was a manuscript. That is the only way you can save yourself.' He stepped closer, but even a full metre away she could feel the red hot end of the branding iron. It looked like he had chosen the one with his initials on it. 'Tell me, can you remember the worst burn you ever had? A careless match, perhaps? A hot pan, fresh off the stove? None of that is comparable to what you are going to feel when I push this iron into your cheek. You will scream until you pass out, and when you come to, you will wish you were dead.'

Jodie held back the tears. 'No! Don't do it!'

Abaddon and Belial laughed. Both of them and the other Disciples were enjoying the show to a sickening degree.

'Then you must do as I ask and tell me everything you know. Who hired you? What does the Creed know? Was there a manuscript? How close are you to de Gama's terrible secret? So many questions, and only when I am satisfied you have answered them all honestly will I order my Disciples to release you.'

'This is insane,' she mumbled, almost passing out with fear. 'It can't be happening.'

He brought the iron right up to her face, forcing a terrified scream from her.

'It's real, Agent Priest. More real than anything you have ever experienced. And it's about to get much, much worse. Now, for the last time... will you tell me what I want to know, or do I have to brand you for life with my initials? Once that happens, you will be my property. Is that what you want?'

Jodie felt her head spinning with terror.

Then, a Disciple entered the room. 'Master, we have a problem.'

The old man spun around. 'What sort of problem?'

'We think the monastery grounds might soon be breached by invaders.'

Razquin nodded and smiled. 'It looks like the cavalry has arrived.'

28

Hunter made one final lap of the monastery with the drone as dusk settled over the land. They'd stopped on their way to the monastery to meet with a CIA man named Agent Jameson. After stashing the relics in a safehouse with him, they had bought the drone. Hunter had flown the small aircraft all over the site in the gloomy, gathering darkness, filming it from every angle with the high-definition onboard camera. Now, they were nestled in the Montserrat mountain range above the monastery. Below them, as they analysed the drone's footage, the moonlight glinted on El Llobregat, the second-longest river in Catalonia.

After a short analysis of the film, they saw the mountain complex had an unusually robust security team for a monastery, at least for tonight. It also helped them see way inside, as well as clocking what looked like a Eurocopter on a newly constructed helipad in the monastery's east cloister.

'Pretty tooled up,' Hunter said. 'Someone in there must be expecting us.'

'And I'm betting most of the monks have no idea what's going on,' said Amy.

'It'll just be the very top,' said Hunter. 'They will have infiltrated the top of the movement and no one below them will have a clue. We saw it before with the Creed's political infiltrations of so many governments around the world.'

'And that means take it easy with the shooting,' Blanco said. 'I like to think we can all tell the difference between an innocent Benedictine monk and an Illuminati cult member, especially if he's holding a submachinegun.'

'Sal's right,' Amy said. 'I don't want any innocent blood lost tonight.'

Hunter said, 'They're probably counting on us having to take so much care. He'll exploit it.'

'I don't care.' Amy doubled down. 'We're not going in there and murdering innocent people. Make sure you have a full positive ID on anyone before you fire. Got it?'

'We got it,' Lewis said. 'And I totally agree.'

After the team decided on the best ingress strategy, they made their move. This involved approaching from the slopes of the Montserrat mountain to the north. This was the best way if they wanted to avoid the heavily armed ring of steel the enemy had positioned around the usual approach by road to the east. Montserrat meant 'serrated mountain' in Catalan, named after the wild, jagged formation of rocks running along its peaks, and it lived up to its name. It was a breathtaking landscape, but also lethal. As they made their way down through narrow, scree-strewn gullies, death was only ever one wrong step away.

Kitted out in the same gear they had used for the Austrian assault, they moved in focused silence along the twisting track until they could see the jumbled rooftops of the eleventh-century monastery dead ahead of them.

'I still see a lot of security,' Quinn said.

'They could just be monks,' said Lewis.

'I don't think so,' said the young goth. 'According to my research, there are around seventy to eighty monks in the monastery. I count at least a dozen just down in that courtyard, and considering it's now full night, my money's on them being Illuminati.'

'Quinn's right,' Amy said. 'But we still have to take it easy. Remember what I said before we climbed down?'

'We do,' Hanna said. 'And I won't be killing anyone, anyway. I refuse to murder.'

Hunter looked at her. 'You might have to defend yourself, Hanna.'

'What happened to Dr Vikander?' she asked with a smile.

He handed her a gun. 'Please, just take this, Hanna. For self-defence if nothing else.'

She reluctantly accepted the weapon.

'So, what now?' Lewis asked. 'I believe this is my first experience raiding a Benedictine monastery so I don't know the etiquette.'

'You haven't raided a Benedictine monastery before?' Hunter said.

'Nope.'

'But you're good with other sorts of monastery?'

The former Marine grinned in the moonlight. 'No, no monasteries. If that makes it clear.'

'As crystal.'

'So, what is the etiquette for storming a monastery?' Quinn said.

'First, don't kill innocent monks,' said Amy. 'I think I might have made that point a second ago.'

Hunter nodded. 'You did, and very well, I thought.'

'Good. Second, remember why we're here. They're holding our friend in there. Jodie is part of this team and she needs our help tonight more than ever. We'll split into two teams when we're inside. Max and I will go find Jodie. Sal, you take Lewis and Quinn and start searching for this Illuminati leader. We're all in radio comms with each other. Stay in contact when possible. We coordinate with each other while we're on the move. Don't stand still for a second. In and out, and that means with both Jodie and their leader if we can get him. We need some answers and he's the man to give them to us. All good?'

Hunter was impressed. 'It really turns me on when you get all "FBI" like this.'

'Max, please,' she said, fighting back a smile. 'Take it seriously.'

'I am taking it seriously. What does FBI stand for again?'

She told him. 'And I know you already know that.'

'I can think of something much sexier than that, though.'

Hanna Vikander sighed. 'Oh, please. Grow up, Maximillian.'

A hawk cried out in the silvery light as Amy fought back a smile. 'I told you to take it seriously.'

'It's Jodie,' he said quietly. 'It's as serious as it gets. But listen, no plan survives contact with the enemy. It's great we have a guide, but when we get in there, we'll have to roll with the punches. C'mon. Let's do it.'

They continued down the slope and stopped at the base of the complex's north wall. They stood still and caught their breath, the night almost totally silent. The wall was too high to climb, but they knew this from the drone reconnoitre. Blanco pulled a grappling hook and rope from his bag and swung it up over the wall. Then, Lewis climbed up the rope and reached the top. He vanished from sight for a few seconds. They heard two boots crunch down on some gravel on the other side of the wall. Footsteps. Silence. Then bolts sliding in the wooden door embedded in the stone wall next to them. It swung open to reveal a smiling Ben Lewis.

'Hey, didn't expect to see you guys here tonight.'

'Funny.' Amy stepped past him and moved into the courtyard. 'See anyone?'

'Not here, but I heard a couple of guys talking around the corner, just behind the tower over there.'

Everyone was inside the courtyard now, guns drawn and ready for action. Moving into the shade of the wall, Amy looked over at the tower Lewis had just described. The large square tower was on their right, in between the basilica where the monks lived and the wide, moonlit Plaça de Santa Maria. Behind the basilica was the main monastery building. Most of the tourist locations, such as the restaurant and cafeteria, were behind them now, also to their right, and further down the slope leading away to the south. Just off to the right of the bell tower, they saw the small roof of the Aeri de Montserrat, the cable car station that brought tourists up to the monastery from another station down by the river in the valley below.

A cursory man-count of Disciples in the courtyard made Hunter doubt himself. 'I only see three or four, at the most. And there are only a few lights on. Maybe we got it wrong. Maybe they didn't bring Jodie here at all.'

'She's here all right,' Amy said. 'I just know it.'

They continued across the courtyard in silence, keeping tight into the shadows of the outer wall until reaching the main complex. In the pale moonlight, they were able to make out an old wooden door embedded in the stone wall of some kind of annex attached to the main part of the monastery. They heard a key rattle in its lock, then the door swung open. Two Disciples stepped out into the courtyard. One of them turned and locked the door.

'When opportunity knocks…' Blanco said. 'Anyone care to join me?'

Hunter was on his feet in a second. The two men crept up behind the Disciples and grabbed hold of them, putting them both in chokeholds and dragging their kicking, squirming bodies back into their cover position behind the outbuilding. Hunter took his out first with a hard strike to the side of the head, knocking him out cold. Blanco increased pressure with his arms and squeezed the man's throat.

'Where's the woman you bastards snatched back in Austria?'

'I don't…' he gasped. 'I don't know.'

'Sure you do, and you've got five seconds to tell me or I'm gonna break your lousy neck.'

He squeezed harder.

'I am not frightened of dying.'

'Good, but I bet you're frightened of your boss. When I find him, I'm going to tell him you told us everything.'

'I'll deny it.'

'Let's give that a try and see how it goes.'

After a pause, the man said, 'She's in the dungeon at the bottom of the monastery. He ordered her to be taken down there when they got a security alert about someone being nearby. But you're too late. The master has already ordered her death. He knows you're here and he no longer needs her alive.'

'And where is the master?'

'At the top of the monastery. There.' He pointed to one of the towers. 'Now, let me…'

Blanco squeezed the man's neck harder until he passed out.

Letting the man's unconscious body slide down to the ground, Blanco reached down and took the key from his pocket. He tossed it in the air and it glinted in the moonlight. 'That's two down and a quiet way into the monastery. You're welcome.'

They crept over to the wooden door and unlocked it, pushing it open. Hunter stepped inside first, followed by Amy, with Blanco, Quinn, and Hanna in the middle and Lewis at the rear. All of them had their guns drawn, ready for anything. They found themselves in a narrow corridor with walls hewn from stone. In some places, open archways led down into darkened corridors. Hush was everywhere. After a long, unsettling hike through the labyrinthine monastery, they all heard a scream break the silence.

'Jodie,' Amy said, her voice breaking. 'That was Jodie.'

29

Hunter led the way to the terrible sound, locating a heavy wooden door at the end of a narrow corridor on their left. The door was open, and Hunter opened it a touch wider before stepping out onto a wooden mezzanine running around a large, great hall, below ground level. A second scream came from a door on the other side of the hall, down on the floor below them.

'We need to get over there,' Hunter said. 'C'mon.'

Placing his feet carefully on a rich, Persian runner to minimise any chances of hitting an errant, squeaking floorboard, he made his way along the narrow walkway running around the top of the hall. The rest of the team followed in his footsteps, guns raised but determined on keeping a low profile until the very last minute.

At the end of the corridor, Hunter paused. He was standing at the top of a flight of stairs leading down into the sunken great hall. Beside him, a candle in an alcove flickered in a draft, and from somewhere below he heard a man praying in Latin. He decided to keep going, and made his way down the steps with the same particular care and attention he had used when searching enemy dwellings in Afghanistan.

At the bottom of the stairs, he crossed the great hall and approached the door from where they thought they had heard the scream. At the door, he raised his right hand and stopped the team. Hunter tested the handle and saw the door was unlocked. He opened it with caution. He'd earned a solid reputation as a leader of troops in the killing fields of Helmand Province during the Afghanistan War, and it was by knowing when to slow down and take stock of a situation. Then he peered through a crack in the door and checked inside. Seeing it was empty, he opened the door wider with his boot and then gestured for the others to follow him inside.

They were in some kind of antechamber. A wooden table was set with a number of votive candles, flickering in the corner and throwing crazy shadows on the plaster wall behind them. On the opposite side of the room was another large, wooden door. It was closed, maybe locked. Hunter stepped forward, gun in hand, and tried the wrought iron ring pull near the lock. Turning it slowly, he heard a click and felt the door pop away from its frame. Then he heard Jodie pleading for her life.

'Like the friendly guy outside just said, she's inside some sort of dungeon,' he said. 'Stone steps are leading down into darkness, but I hear her voice. She's in real trouble.'

Blanco bristled. 'Not for long. The only people in trouble are the assholes trying to hurt her.'

Hunter silently agreed and made his way down the stone steps, keeping to the side, up against the stone wall until he reached a landing. Here, he paused and peered around the corner in the staircase. What he saw made his blood run cold. One of the Disciples was holding Jodie, gripping her by her neck and forcing her toward another room.

'Stay calm. We're almost there,' Hunter said. 'Stay alert.'

'Make sure your weapons are ready,' said Amy. 'And well done. We did it. We found her.'

'Let's not celebrate too soon,' said Blanco. 'She's still in danger and those guys are spoiling for a fight, for damned sure.'

Their voices quietened down as they watched the Disciple dragging Jodie into the other room. Her hands and feet were bound together and she was gagged. The man positioned her at the side of a pool, littered with floating candles. Above it, on the wall, a large rendering of the Eye of Providence was painted in red on a white wall. A man standing by a roaring fire laughed at the proceedings. He looked like someone with something to celebrate, and Blanco was right; the Disciples surrounding them were ready for anything.

'If they're spoiling for a fight,' Hunter said, 'then let's give them one to remember.'

Hunter wasted no time in launching the assault. With the rest of the team at his side, he charged down the final few steps, gun in hand and screaming at the men to stop what they were doing to Jodie, but it was too late. One of them pushed her into the water. Bound and gagged, she fell forward helplessly and crashed through the surface, disappearing from sight.

The men scrambled to defend their leader, forming a human wall around the master and reaching for their guns. Amy, Hanna, Quinn, and Lewis fixed their guns on them.

'Freeze!' Amy yelled. 'Guns on the floor and kick them over here. Then get your hands in the air where I can see them.'

The Disciples looked at their master for guidance. He nodded once and they obeyed. After a clattering of weapons on the stone floor, they kicked them across to Amy and the others and raised their hands. Behind her, Hunter and Blanco were pulling Jodie from the water.

'Is she going to be all right, Max?' Amy asked, momentarily taking her eyes away from the master and his Disciples to watch them pulling Jodie up onto the flagstone floor.

Hunter said nothing. He was checking her pulse and airway. Then he began mouth-to-mouth resuscitation. The sound of his breathing into her mouth as he tried to stimulate respiration sent a shiver up Amy's spine.

'Max?'

'He's working on it, Amy,' Blanco said. The big man looked past Amy at the master. 'And if he fails, you die next.'

'I don't understand how you got here,' the master said, ignoring the threat. 'But I understand you have made a grave error in coming here tonight. This is a sacred place and this was a special moment for us. A sacrifice to the divine force we worship. You have broken the sanctity of one of our most holy rituals.'

Amy's face contorted into a rictus of contempt. For a second, she found it hard to find her voice. 'One of your rituals? That's my friend over there. Somebody's daughter.'

The master smiled. 'Meaningless.'

Hunter thought he had lost Jodie. Army training had taught him that

CPR worked up to six minutes after a heart had stopped. He knew Jodie had been out less than a minute. But she was not responding. With interlocked fingers, he started the chest compressions, two inches down and one hundred compressions per minute.

'Max?'

'It's too late,' the master said quietly. 'She is already serving our Dark Lord.'

Quinn took a step back. 'These guys are even crazier than the Creed.'

When Amy heard Jodie spluttering back to life, she felt a wave of relief wash over her like a tsunami. 'Thank God,' she mumbled under her breath.

'Are you okay?' Hunter asked, checking her eyes and lifting her up off the floor. He began cutting the tape holding her hands and feet together.

'What the hell happened?' Jodie asked.

'They almost killed you,' Blanco said. 'By drowning.'

Her eyes widened, but she was still woozy. She took a deep breath and coughed again. 'Please tell me you didn't bring the relics.' She caught a knowing glance shared by Amy and Blanco. 'Oh, damn it.'

'We had no choice,' Amy said. 'But they're hidden. If you think I value a bunch of gold artifacts more than your life, you don't know me very well. Not even a city of gold is worth a single life.'

'Damn it, Amy! They're not after gold. It's something else.'

The master laughed. 'Indeed, it is something else, something altogether different. More powerful than any amount of gold. But you do not need to worry about any of this. There is no way you can escape this monastery. There are too many of us. Too many Disciples, everywhere you go.'

'What about the monks?' Amy asked. 'Do they know about what you're doing here?'

'There are no monks. We took over this place a few days ago and killed them all. This is our place now. Another supreme being is worshipped here now. You can forget about any monks coming to your assistance.'

'But I saw them.'

'No, you saw Disciples dressed as monks.'

Blanco said, 'You can't hope to get away with this.'

'The Illuminati don't "get away with things", Mr Blanco. We are everything. If we decide to slaughter the monks in this monastery and use it as our home, then that is made so. There are no questions from any quarter.

We control all. You will die here tonight, and your bodies will be burned, the same fate as befell the monks.'

'Then you're not going to get your relics,' Hunter said, standing up. 'Because they're somewhere you arseholes will never find them. The only way you get them is if we're allowed free passage out of here. That's the deal. You kill us and you lose any hope of finding El Dorado.'

A broad smile spread across the master's face. 'You mean these relics?'

He snapped his fingers and Belial pulled a bag out from behind the table by the fire. He handed them to the master. The master then pulled the crucifix from the bag. He smiled further and brought the other relics out.

'And yes, Agent Jameson is dead and the safehouse is burned to the ground.'

Amy felt her stomach turn. 'You sons of bitches. How did you know?'

'We worship the All-Seeing Eye for a good reason. More than that, you have no need to know. Now, lower your weapons and I will make your executions instant and painless. If you make my Disciples chase you all over the monastery, I'll show you something that makes the Creed's chimera look like a Burmese kitten.'

'I guess I'll just take that risk,' Amy, said, turning her head and looking at her friends. 'Right, guys?'

'Right,' Blanco said. 'Let's get out of here.'

Without guns, the master and the Disciples were helpless and could do nothing but watch as Amy and her team retraced their steps back up the stone staircase and through the door. Blanco slammed it shut and turned the key.

'That won't keep them for long,' he said.

'We're already busted,' Quinn said, pointing at the stone staircase on the other side of the hall. Half a dozen Disciples were running down from a higher floor, guns in hand, robes flowing out behind them. They opened fire on them. Bullets pinged off the wall and blew chunks of stone dust over them.

'This way,' Lewis said. 'I know a way out of this madhouse. I saw it on the way up the mountain.'

With the Disciples at their back, he led the team through a maze of corridors. He never lost his focus. Recalling his US Marine training, he kept a cool head and slowly made his way through the labyrinthine monastery until reaching an outside door. Stepping into the night, he took stock and found east. 'This way!'

'Where are we going?' Amy asked.

'To take advantage of some free air miles supplied by Illuminati Air.'

'The chopper!' Quinn said. 'Good call. You can fly that type, right, Sal?'

Blanco nodded. 'Sure can.'

He led them out to the courtyard where they had seen the chopper. Safely inside and engine spooling up, Blanco lifted the aircraft up off the ground just as the yard flooded with Disciples, guns firing. He rotated the helicopter as fast as the model's specs allowed and nipped down over the perimeter wall, bullets flying left and right of them.

'That was too close,' Amy said.

'And they're not going to stop coming after us,' said Hunter.

'But they've already seen the relics,' Jodie said. 'They would have made photos of the symbols.'

'Sure, but they're going to want their helicopter back, right?' he said with a smile.

Amy frowned. 'Hanna, you need to get to work on the last symbols and find out what they mean.'

'So, where's our next stop after that?' Hanna asked.

Amy furrowed her brow, a look of nervous tension spreading on her face. 'I think we all know where our next stop is going to be.'

30

'The *Seawolf*!'

Hunter was startled by Amy's sudden exclamation. He turned in his seat, working hard not to look at all impressed by it all. Barcelona was already twelve hours behind them, and the deep azure water of the North Atlantic now spread out below, sparkling in the bright marine sunshine.

High above the Newfoundland Ridge, nearly four hundred miles from the coast of Newfoundland, their chopper had only just enough fuel to turn around and return home if it failed to make the rendezvous. Today, that contingency would not be necessary. Oskar Rorschach's enormous underwater yacht, the *Seawolf*, was exactly where they had expected to find it, cutting west through the water at what couldn't have been any faster than a leisurely ten knots or so.

'At least we won't have to land at sea then,' said Hunter.

Amy smiled. It felt good to have her whole team back under her wing, all safe and sound. Jodie's close call back in Spain had unsettled her more than she'd expected and made her ask some personal questions about whether Jodie and Quinn should be out in the field on active missions.

Her thoughts were ended by the chopper swinging hard to the left as the pilot made a sharp turn and descended rapidly towards the sea. A few seconds later, they were landing on the *Seawolf*'s helipad at the back of the enormous submarine yacht. Touched down, they filed out of the helicopter and were met by a member of Rorschach's crew. He whisked them inside the boat and straight to the bridge.

The bearded Rorschach was wearing a white Merino wool submariner roll neck and blue jeans. He greeted them with a loud 'hello' and opened his arms. 'Welcome back to the *Seawolf*! So good to see you all.'

As Amy and Hunter shook his hand, Quinn took one look at the jumper and smiled. 'All he needs is a Dixie cup hat and a corncob pipe and he's away.'

Blanco shushed her, but couldn't resist a smile of his own. 'That's enough, Q,' he whispered. 'We're Mr Rorschach's guests and we're very lucky to have the use of his yacht.'

'Sure, but if at any point he calls me "me hearty", I'm outta here, Sal.'

'He just takes his sailing seriously,' Blanco said, still smiling. 'That's all.'

Rorschach walked over to them and now shook their hands. 'It's so good to have you on board. I can't say how excited I was to learn that you wanted me to take you down to the *Titanic*. It's something I have always wanted to do. In fact, it's one of the reasons I designed this submarine to be able to withstand pressures of that depth. But UNESCO has denied me permission to visit the site on more than one occasion so this is a dream come true for me. It's a match made in heaven!'

Jodie looked at him with some concern. 'Will we be able to go in the wreck in diving suits?'

Rorschach smiled. 'No. The best ADS technology vessels we have today have crush depths of two thousand feet,' Rorschach said glumly. 'Considering the *Titanic* is twelve and half thousand feet down, you'll understand why when we're down there we have to use the submersibles and drones. Maybe one day we might have the ability to walk around in deep-sea wrecks, but not today.'

Amy understood. 'I'm not sure I'd want to be so deep in a glorified diving suit anyway.'

Rorschach laughed. 'ADS tech is a little more complicated than that, but I can understand your concerns. And I realise we have more concerns than deep-sea diving.'

'Yes,' Amy said. 'We're not the only ones searching for El Dorado. There are two other groups in the search. The Creed you already know, and now there's a second group claiming to be the Illuminati. Take it from me, they're even worse than the Creed.'

Rorschach was shocked. 'The Creed almost killed us all during the Atlantis mission, Amy. You say this other group is even more dangerous?'

'I think so, yes.'

'And they could be on their way here right now,' Hunter said.

'Both groups?' Rorschach asked.

Hunter nodded. 'We've seen all four discovered relics and so have the Illuminati. The Creed only saw three because they never got their hands on the crucifix in Barcelona. But that's beside the point, which is that both groups know the fifth idol is almost certainly down at the *Titanic*'s wreck site.'

Rorschach drew a long breath and gave a knowing nod. 'In this case, we have no time to spare. You must meet the twins at once.'

Amy was confused. 'The twins?'

Rorschach chuckled and clapped her on the shoulder. 'Come along, my dear. I'll introduce you to them now.'

31

The twins turned out to be the Nerthus and Nehalennia, two fierce-looking mini-submersibles designed specifically for deep-sea salvage work by Rorschach himself. Named after a Norse god and goddess associated with the sea, they were small, black metal spheres, covered with robotic arms and bolt-on LED lights.

'What's the average life expectancy for someone who gets in one of those things?' Jodie asked with a frown. 'Twenty minutes, or ten?'

Rorschach laughed. 'They're perfectly safe. Only a dozen of my men perished inside them during the testing phase.'

She looked at him, horror slowly dawning on her face.

'I'm joking, Agent Priest!'

'Thank God for that.'

His smile faded. 'In fact, it was only six men.'

'Damn it, Oskar,' Amy said. 'Can't you see she's terrified? I am too, by the way.'

He laughed. 'There is no need to fear anything. Only one of them is functional at this time, as the other was damaged on a mission in the Mediterranean a few days ago. But we need them. You see, the *Seawolf* can only get us so far. After a certain point, the pressure becomes too great even for her and we need to switch to one of the twins. Or you do, I should say! They are necessary for another reason, as well. The *Seawolf* is far too large to get inside the wreck and explore. For that, we need these much smaller and more mobile vehicles. Nerthus and Nehalennia are perfect for this. Don't worry about trying to remember all that. Now you've been introduced, you can call them N1 and N2, just like everyone else aboard the *Seawolf*. You will be traveling in the N1.'

After a long silence in the submersible bay, Amy cleared her throat. 'This is going to be very dangerous and none of us has had training in this area. Please, Oskar, we need to know the risks.'

As the *Seawolf* rolled in the sea, Rorschach gave an honest answer. 'Yes, it's dangerous, of course it is. All underwater work carries inherent risk, and at the depths we're talking about, the risks grow exponentially. Down on the floor of the Atlantic is not a place you're supposed to be, at all. The pressure down there will crush you like the proverbial grape. The only thing stopping that from happening is the reinforced hulls of the Nerthus and the Nehalennia. Down there, N1 is the only thing between you and the most horrible death you can imagine.'

'Whoa,' Jodie said. 'Enough with all the optimism.'

'I'm sorry, but Amy asked me to explain the dangers and I want to be honest. If anything happens to the N1 when you're down there, there is absolutely zero chance of survival. You need to know this when you're assessing risk down there. Besides, you'll be with Jens, my best sailor.'

Jens slapped Hunter on the back. 'And let's get this party started, partner! Who are my travelling companions today?'

'How many fit inside?' Amy asked.

'Three.'

'Well, I'm one of them,' she said. 'I'm not sending anyone down there if I'm not prepared to go myself.'

'And me,' Hunter said. 'No doubts. I'm the best qualified to identify the idol if we should be so lucky to find it.'

'Then that's agreed,' Jens said. 'Let's do it.'

Hunter pocketed his doubts for later, climbed up to the top of N1 and lowered himself down just as he had seen Jens do. Getting through the small hatch was tight, but when he was inside there was a little more room than he had anticipated. Jens was already strapping himself into one of the two front seats.

Hunter did the same as Amy climbed down and sat in the seat behind them. The interior was mostly smooth metal and rivets with a panel of glowing instruments at the front. There were no windows, but a large computer screen that relayed information fed into it by various cameras fixed to the craft's exterior.

'So this is what it feels like to be inside a submarine inside a submarine,' Hunter said with an unsettled glance at Jens. 'Nice.'

'Yeah, really cosy,' Amy said, fitting her belt. 'And not claustrophobic at all.'

Jens laughed. 'You either get used to it or you don't. I've spent most of my adult life under the waves. First in the Norwegian Navy's submarine fleet, most recently on the *Utsira*, and now with Mr Rorschach. It suits me.'

'Not me,' Amy said. 'Give me terra firma every time.'

'There's really nothing to be concerned about,' Jens said calmly. 'We'll go down into the water and drop away from the hull of the *Seawolf* and then make our way down to the wreck. We'll be monitored the whole time by the *Seawolf*. Then we'll go into the wreck in the steerage area and use the remote submarine drone fixed to our hull to search for the idol. That's it. With some luck, we'll locate the idol and then after bringing the drone back to N1, we'll simply ascend back up to the *Seawolf*. Then it's showers and a good hearty meal. Mr Rorschach might even break out the brandy if the mission is a success.'

'You make it sound so simple,' Hunter said. 'Unfortunately, I'm too much of a cynic to think anything can go that much to plan.'

'Ah, a pessimist. I sailed on the *Utsira* with a man like that. Glass half empty. We called him the Cautious Admiral because he was always so careful. Convinced everything always went wrong for him.'

'And don't tell me,' Amy said. 'He retired to the Caribbean and lived happily ever after.'

'No, he was killed in a horrific diving accident. You don't want to know the details.'

Hunter and Amy exchanged a glance. 'Thanks for that, Chief,' Hunter said.

Jens gave a deep belly laugh and began flipping switches on the panel in front of him. 'No problem at all. Just trying to make everything mellow in here. A little submariner humour.' He slipped his headset on and pulled a retractable microphone down to his lips. '*Seawolf*, come in, please. *Seawolf*, are you reading me?'

'This is the *Seawolf*, we're receiving you.'

'Good job. Let's hope we have a good dive today.'

Rorschach's voice was clear but weak in the small speakers inside their sub. 'And get us that little idol I've been hearing so much about. Can't wait to see it.'

'That makes two of us,' Hunter said. 'I must admit, the archaeologist in me is pretty excited about this one.'

* * *

Hunter's excitement about the potential archaeological discovery at the end of the dive was gradually replaced with fear and trepidation the deeper the N1 descended. It was bad enough being inside a small, windowless metal sphere with only a computer screen to see what was outside, but even worse when the screen flickered on and off.

'Just a small hitch with the cameras,' Jens said in a reassuring tone. 'At these depths, they're under intense pressure. Don't worry, they'll be fine.'

'That's great,' Amy said. 'But I'm more interested in our safety.'

'We'll be fine too,' he said. 'Just relax and enjoy the view. We should be seeing our first glimpse of the wreck very soon. It's a moment you'll remember for the rest of your life.'

Hunter blinked as he stared into the monitor above the panel. Just a black void lit by two yellow arc lights, slowly receding into the darkness. Occasionally, what looked like a dust mote drifted past them. Other than that, there was nothing at all out there.

'It's blacker than space,' Amy said.

Hunter agreed. 'Not much to see yet.'

Jens smiled. 'Be patient. We're almost there. We'll be running into the *Titanic* any second now.'

'But what if we run into something else first?' Amy said.

'Like what?' Jens said, turning to face her briefly. 'A giant squid?'

'No, the Creed,' she said flatly. 'Or the Illuminati. They're not without resources, Jens. If Oskar Rorschach can afford to put together an operation like this, then so can they. They want this idol even more than we do.'

'What you say may be true,' Jens said calmly. 'But they're not down here now, for sure.' He tapped a dial in front of his chair just behind the steering yoke. 'This is the state-of-the-art sonar and it's not giving me any indication of anything down here with us except the wreck. Not only that, the sonar on the *Seawolf* showed the area was clear on our way to meet you, as did the radar when we were on the surface. You do not need to be worried about an attack from anyone.'

'I wish I could share your optimism,' she said.

Jens adjusted the controls and they all felt the submersible descend faster. 'Where exactly are we going when we get there, Max?'

Hunter said, 'According to the letter Bauer had, Jeremiah said his steerage cabin was on the ship's starboard side, just below the fourth smokestack on E Deck. It was at the stern of a long passageway the passengers used to call Scotland Road, after a street in Liverpool. It's too narrow for the NI, but fear not! That's what the drone is for, right?'

Jens nodded. 'Correct.'

Amy jumped as the side of the NI scraped against the hull of the *Titanic*. 'What's happening?'

'Sorry,' Jens said, correcting his course. 'A slight navigation error. We got a little too close to the seabed.'

'Are we damaged?' Hunter asked.

'Not at all. The NI can take more much more of a beating than that.'

Hunter prayed he was right as the NI's forward lights illuminated the seabed in front of them. He was surprised to see they were still only a few metres above it, despite Jens's correction, and travelling much faster than he had imagined. He leaned closer to the computer screen and stared at the bottom of the Atlantic in wonder. So few people had seen this with their own eyes, he felt genuinely privileged and a little awestruck. Then his mouth fell open in shock as he finally saw the wreck.

Behind him, Amy gasped. 'That's incredible.'

'It's quite a sight, no?' Jens said.

Hunter stared into the screen, speechless. His career as an army officer and a UNESCO field archaeologist had given him many amazing experiences, and many unforgettable sights, but this was something he instantly knew was uniquely special. Seeing the great black wall of the ship's starboard side rising up in front of him, the same ship he had seen so many times before in endless pictures and old films, was shocking. Everything looked different. First, it was covered in rusticles and barnacles wherever he looked. Worse, it was badly crumpled from the impact on the seafloor, rendering it almost unrecognisable. It was at once a breathtaking and tragic sight.

'I'm impressed,' he said.

'I'm speechless,' said Amy.

Jens smiled again. 'And I'm going to park up and get the drone out.'

32

Hunter took a breath and tried to remain calm as the Norwegian turned his seat until he was facing the sidewall and a second instrument panel. He locked the seat into its new position and began to fire up the drone. A second computer screen flickered to life, showing a live feed from the drone's camera, and then they all felt a deep clunk as the drone detached from the N1's hull.

'We're on the move,' Jens said. 'Everybody, stay tuned for the most exciting adventure of their lives!'

'You're like a kid in a candy store,' Amy said with a smile.

'Can you blame me? My entire life is the sea and salvaging wrecks. Having the opportunity to drive a drone through the corridors of the *Titanic* is a dream come true. I guess you could say it's the high point of my whole career. I can't imagine what could ever top this.'

Hunter peered at the small screen over Jens's shoulder as he watched in amazement as the drone's light shone on the wreck's hull. Jens found a long gouge in the side of the vessel, which must have torn open when the ship crashed into the seafloor, and carefully piloted the drone towards it.

Hunter and Amy exchanged an excited glance as Jens navigated the drone through the hole and inside the wreck. 'I can hardly believe I'm seeing this in real-time,' Amy said.

A tinny, metallic pinging sound filled the cabin. Jens darted his head towards the main panel.

'What was that?' Amy asked.

'A sonar pulse,' Jens said, confused. 'I don't understand.'

Hunter looked at the sonar panel. They all heard a second ping as the green sonar screen flickered in the dimly lit cabin.

'And another.' Jens brought the drone down onto the corridor floor and turned his seat back to its original position. 'It seems like there are some kind of vessels inside the ship's hull, and also some further back on the outside behind the stern. But this is impossible.'

'Maybe it's malfunctioning,' Amy said with a nervous laugh.

'No,' Jens said. 'We have company. It looks like you may have been right about the Creed after all. I'm reading one more craft approaching from the east. Smaller than the ones inside the ship but similar in size to the N1. Travelling about the same speed we're capable of.'

'This is not good,' Hunter said.

'No,' said Jens, his voice trailing into a tense silence. 'We must continue with the mission and secure the idol before they get here. I think we have time.'

'How much time do we have?' Amy asked.

'Maybe ten minutes.'

'Will that be enough?' asked Hunter.

'I think so.'

'What about the other pings you got from inside the wreck?' Amy asked.

'They're static, and do not appear to be a threat to us at this time. We're almost at Jeremiah's cabin now. Look.'

Hunter watched as Jens raised the drone from the corridor floor and increased speed until the drone reached the end of Scotland Road. The eerie, underwater passageway commanded respect from all of them as they each imagined the number of people who'd once walked up and down it. Now, nothing but black water and floating debris kicked up by the drone's powerful propellers.

The sonar pinged again.

'The larger craft to the east is getting closer,' Jens said. 'Amy, you'd better report the situation to the *Seawolf*. Use the radio kit just off to your right.'

'On it.'

'Tell them we're going into Jeremiah's cabin but we have potential hostiles in the vicinity.'

'I think we could lose the "potential" bit,' Hunter said. 'They're hardly likely to be harmless tourists out on an excursion for the day. It's either the Creed or the Illuminati, for sure, and we could be in real trouble if they're armed.'

As Amy radioed up to the *Seawolf*, Jens said, 'What number was his cabin again, Max?'

Hunter looked down at the letter. 'Number three. According to this deck plan, we're almost there.'

Jens piloted the drone into a cramped, junk-filled cabin and rotated it left and right to get a good overview of everything. On the floor, they saw old ceramic mugs, bowls, a leather boot, and what looked like a comb, all poking up from a thick layer of grey silt. All strewn over the floor exactly where they landed over one hundred years ago. 'Looks like we made it, but we don't have long to look for the idol.'

Amy finished her call up to the *Seawolf*. 'Bad news. That was Sal. He said they've come under attack up there from a large vessel dropping depth charges. They've had to take evasive action and dive even deeper to avoid the charges.'

'Damn it,' Hunter said. 'This is spinning rapidly out of control.'

'There!' Amy called out, making both men jump. 'In the corner, I see some kind of bag.'

Jens drove the drone into the corner of the small cabin and shone the light downwards. In the silt, they all saw the opening of what looked like some kind of leather bag. The drone's propellers kicked up more and more of the silt and clouded their view. In the gloom, the light struck something reflective.

'That's it!' said Amy. 'It has to be.'

'I think we found what we're searching for,' Jens said, relief obvious in his voice. He grabbed the idol and turned the drone back to the N1. Moments later they heard a clunking sound as it fixed back onto the hull.

Then the N1 rocked violently to one side and began to tip over in the water.

Hunter grabbed hold of the instrument panel to keep himself in his seat. 'And I think the Illuminated Ones just found us.'

Amy's eyes turned frantically to Jens. 'What do we do?'

The Norwegian was calm under fire. 'We get back to Mother, fast.'

Spotlights flashed in Amy's eyes as Jens tried to turn the N1 and rammed the thrusters to full power. The other sub's steel claws scraped down their hull as it tried to grab hold of them. Its engines revved and produced a wild storm of bubbles as its driver maneuvered closer to them, striking out with the claws all over again.

'Take that, bastards,' Jens said, slamming the portside throttle lever down and spinning the N1 around into the other sub. The collision was hard and fast, a loud metallic clanging sound reverberating around inside the N1.

'What happened?' Amy asked.

Jens completed the turn 'I don't know, but our forward camera should pick them up soon.'

Hunter scanned the screens. 'I don't see a thing.'

'There!' Amy pointed in the corner of the screen. 'I see the other sub. It's tumbling down inside the *Titanic*'s wreck.'

'Oh dear, what a shame,' Jens said, peering closely at the screen and squinting. 'It appears my little manoeuvre damaged their ballast tanks. Looks like they're on a one-way trip to the bottom of the Atlantic. They'll all die in the wreck.'

Amy looked at Hunter. He shrugged. 'Oskar said Jens was the best.'

'I paid him to say that,' said the Norwegian, steering them back to the sub. 'Wait, we have another problem.'

'What is it?'

'The *Seawolf* is already on the surface. Something must have happened.'

'We have nowhere else to go,' Hunter said.

'Max is right,' said Jens. 'We must go up into the docking bay, whatever happens. We are running very low on oxygen.'

The small team waited in grim silence for a surprise attack from another submersible as they forced air from their tanks and rose up to the *Seawolf*, but none came.

A few metres from the giant submarine yacht, Amy sighed. 'Looks like we made it.'

'Don't speak so soon,' Hunter said. 'We don't know what's going on up top yet.'

Jens's face hardened as he brought the N1 into the docking bay. 'No, we don't.'

33

Hunter watched as Jens spun open the escape hatch wheel and pushed the thick metal disc open. Artificial light streamed down onto the Norwegian sailor's face, followed by a hail of bullets that ripped into him and blasted him back inside the submersible with horrific, fatal wounds.

Amy screamed as Hunter reached down and pulled the dead man's body out of the way of the small ladder leading up to the hatch. Then he snatched the pistol from Jens's hand and returned fire through the hatch. He heard a scream, but then more shots. More than one of them up there, he thought. He fired again but missed. Peering through a gap by the hatch's hinges, he saw a man tearing the idol from the side of the N1.

'Damn it, they got the idol.'

'What do we do now?' Amy asked. 'Not only do they have the idol, but we're literally fish in a damned barrel.'

'Not literally,' he said. 'Fish can't do this.'

He fired another shot and the men outside returned fire. He put his finger to Amy's lips and then screamed in pain, faking a terrible bullet wound. Seconds later, a face appeared in the open hatch, and Hunter fired, killing the man instantly. The docking bay fell silent.

'Quick, follow me,' he said, climbing up the ladder and peering quickly over the top. 'We're clear for now, but I can hear footsteps heading this way. We haven't got long.'

Up top, things got worse fast. The man he had shot was still holding the idol. Hunter grabbed it and threw it to Amy. 'You got your phone?'

'Uh-huh.'

'Grab a picture, now.'

She did it, then stashed it in her bag. Then they heard footsteps. The footsteps turned into countless enemy soldiers streaming into the docking bay. Gunshots rang out in the yacht's docking bay and bullets pinged off the vessel's smooth metal hull in showers of sparks. Hunter saw men running to offensive positions and heard yelling as they helped each other advance towards the N1 at the end of the bay.

They climbed off the sub and ran to the nearest exit hatch when yet more soldiers ran into the docking bay and opened fire on them alongside the others. One of the men let rip with a submachinegun and showered them in a hail of bullets, forcing them to dive for cover behind one of the bay's steel davit cranes. The automatic gunfire continued, blasting paint off the steel hull above their heads.

'They're keeping us pinned down,' Hunter said. 'Expect another advance any second.'

More gunfire from the other side of the docking bay. Hunter looked around the side of the crane to see how far the men had moved towards their position but was surprised to see two of them tumbling into the water, riddled with bullet holes. Behind the men's position, he saw two of Rorschach's crew and Jodie running into the bay from one of the hatches at the other end.

'Looks like the cavalry has arrived,' he said.

'Huh?'

'Jodie and some new friends. And just in time, too. Now we have the enemy in a pincer movement. Let's go!'

She ducked for the cover of the davit crane, then ran along the side of the docking bay behind the submersible. Amy opened the farthest hatch and kicked it open, gun at the ready. The corridor on the other side of the hatch was all clear. 'We're good this way.'

Hunter waved Jodie through into the corridor, firing on the last Creed soldier to give both her and Amy the cover they needed to get out of the docking bay. Then he darted through the hatch, bullets ricocheting on the steel hull all around him. He emerged into the corridor, cursing and shouting, to find Amy and Jodie already making their way towards a ladder at the end. Up top, somewhere several decks above their current position, they all heard another deep, growling roar. The *Seawolf* rocked from side to side, almost knocking them off their feet.

Amy reached out and grabbed a rail running along the corridor wall. 'Damn it! What the hell is going on up there?'

'It's a full-on attempt to make us surrender,' Jodie said.

Amy climbed the ladder, gun in one hand. Hunter felt a pang of nerves as he watched her go up ahead of him, but she was a highly trained FBI agent and knew what she was doing. He didn't like it, but he pushed his worries away and said nothing. As a former Guards officer in the British Army, he knew better than to second-guess and question the skills and bravery of other well-trained soldiers.

'It's all clear up here, too!' they heard Amy say.

'You're next, Jodie. I'll cover you.'

She nodded and made the short climb. Jodie's skills were many, but she wasn't trained in close-quarter combat the way Hunter was and she knew it. It was just as well. Halfway up the ladder, a soldier burst through the hatch at the other end of the corridor and opened fire on them. Hunter had expected it and had trained his gun on the open hatch just in case. The second the man appeared there, he fired three shots into his head and blasted him up against the end of the corridor, blood spraying all over the steel.

He whirled around and made his way up behind Jodie as fast as he could go. If anyone else came through that hatch in support of their fallen comrade, he'd be taking a dozen rounds direct in his back and there'd be nothing he could do to stop it. As it happened, he made it to the top in one piece, out of breath and heart pounding in his chest.

They were standing in another corridor but this time in the top half of the yacht. The floor was carpeted and the space was decorated with plants and pictures. Amy had already figured out the best way up to the *Seawolf*'s control room and was making her way up a flight of stairs, gun once again at the ready.

'It's up here,' she called out. 'I remember it.'

She signalled for the other two to follow her with a wave of her other hand. Another explosion rocked the ship. Hunter heard agonised screams from someplace up top and prayed they were the enemy and not Rorschach's crew or HARPA. After the second explosion, the whole of *Seawolf* began to list even more heavily to port. As he ran up the stairs behind Jodie, everything was tipped over at forty-five degrees, reminding him of some crazy horror film.

'This is not conducive to running along a corridor,' he called out, one foot on the floor and another on the bottom of the wall. 'At all.'

'Just keep going, Hunter,' Jodie called out. 'Show us all what a hero you can be when the chips are down.'

Hunter had a ready reply but kept it to himself. On a joint service training mission in the Arctic, he'd had to meet with a Norwegian submariner who had told him about an accident on a Russian submarine he'd heard about. No news coverage, but the details were horrific. After a serious accident on board, the vessel had ended up on the floor of the Baltic Sea and a fire had broken out. It turned out that sometimes reality was worse than anything summoned by the imagination, and sometimes when Hunter recalled the Norwegian's details of what had happened down there, he felt like he needed a strong drink. The young thief from California didn't need that sort of movie running in her head.

'We're there!' Amy yelled from above them.

He joined Jodie and Amy at the top of the stairs. They were on the main deck containing the control room and most of the sleeping quarters. He smelled gunpowder and burning plastic. A thin layer of smoke was hanging in the air just above head height. He thought he heard the roaring pop and crackle of flames. A klaxon roared.

'This is all really bad,' he said. 'We need to find the others and get out of here as fast as we can.'

As he spoke, a tall man with a shaved head and tattoos on his neck whirled into view around the corner right in front of them. He was holding an automatic rifle, but it was pointing to the ground and at arm's reach. A rookie mistake, Hunter thought, and he kicked the weapon from his grip with a hefty smack of his boot before bringing the back of his fist up and smashing it into his tattooed neck.

The startled man staggered back and reached for a two-way radio on his belt. He'd just about brought it up to his mouth to speak into it when

Hunter belted that away too. Then he headbutted him and knocked him to the ground, blood all over his face.

Hunter reached up and rubbed his forehead. 'Damn, damn, damn and buggeration that hurt! Damn!'

The man scrambled over to the rifle Hunter had booted out of his hands, but Amy fired into him with her handgun, burying two rounds into his midriff. The man's substantial body ploughed into the carpet like a downed bomber, arms spread out at odd angles on either side of him. He expelled his last breath as Amy brought the gun down, slightly shaking, in her hand.

'Good work, boss,' Jodie said. 'That sack of shit was about to rip us all to pieces.'

Amy said nothing. She looked at the dead man for another second and then moved on. 'All right, we keep going. This way to the control room. Let's just pray our friends are all still alive.'

* * *

Blanco was up to his neck in water. Freezing cold Atlantic saltwater. Tipping his head back to stop it from forcing its way into his mouth and down into his lungs, he grabbed hold of a steel roof beam and heaved himself up towards an escape hatch in the ceiling.

Lewis was already climbing through, and out of immediate danger. Now, the younger man threw his arm down and gripped Blanco's hand.

The two men had been down in the torpedo room helping some of Rorschach's sailors load torpedoes into the tubes ready for firing when they got to the surface. They didn't know exactly what was up there, but whatever it was had to be sunk as fast as possible if they were to stand half a chance of survival. Then, on their way up to the surface, something, maybe a chopper, had deployed a series of depth charges all around their position. Rorschach had done well to avoid most, but the latest one had been almost a direct hit. Now, water was flooding into their deck, filling the engine and torpedo rooms with icy water.

'That was close,' Blanco yelled over the warning klaxon as Lewis pulled him up out of the torpedo room.

'You can say that again,' Lewis said as he slammed the hatch shut and locked it as fast as possible.

'Yeah,' Blanco said gruffly. 'A little too close for Smith and Richardson.' Both men had been killed in the blast, and now their bodies were trapped in the flooded room below the hatch. 'We need to get back to the control room.'

They sprinted through the underwater yacht's labyrinthine passageways and stairwells until they reached the *Seawolf*'s nerve centre. Rorschach was at the periscope, cursing. His sailors hurriedly moved back and forth, operating radios and sonars and radars. The sense of chaos was further increased by the sub listing heavily to port. In the mayhem, Blanco spotted Jodie and Quinn sitting out of the way just behind Rorschach.

In front of them, Brodie McCabe was holding a gun and the bag full of relics.

Hunter stepped towards him. 'Brodie, you bastard.'

'Tut tut, Max,' McCabe said, rotating to point the gun momentarily at him instead. 'Take a step back or take a bullet through the stomach.'

'He's not kidding, Max,' Quinn said. 'He already shot and killed two sailors.'

'And I'll happily do the same to all of you, too,' McCabe said. 'Unless you hand over that idol.'

Hunter looked at Amy. They knew they had no choice.

He held out the idol. 'Why not come and get it, Brodie?'

'I think not. Drop it on the floor and kick it over here. Now.'

'You're not going to get away with this,' Hunter said. 'And now the Illuminati are hunting you down, too.'

McCabe huffed out a disrespectful snort. 'You leave worrying about that to me.'

'You won't get very far with it,' Hanna said. 'It took me hours to translate de Gama's cipher.'

Hunter winced. 'Damn it, Hanna.'

The Swede looked at him, confused, but McCabe was a step ahead. 'Excellent, Dr Vikander. My most sincere thanks to you. I was going to invite Max here to join us onboard the *Hermes*, but it appears you are the expert we're looking for.'

'Wait,' she said, looking to Max. 'I didn't mean—'

'Step over to the ladder,' McCabe said. 'Right now.'

'Do as he says, Hanna,' Hunter said. 'Or he's going to kill one of us.'

McCabe laughed, picked up the idol and put it in the bag with the other relics, and then ordered Hanna up the conning tower ladder. 'I don't know where the Alumbrados is, but I know where you are, or at least where you're going, and that's right to the bottom of the sea. You can spend your last few minutes suffocating in this yacht as it slowly sinks down to the wreck. Meanwhile, I'll be discovering de Gama's Golden One. Goodbye.'

'You can't do this to us, Brodie!' Hunter yelled.

It was useless. McCabe was already following Hanna up the ladder. Then his two bodyguards turned and followed him up. When they slammed the hatch shut, the noise seemed to echo for hours.

'You all okay?' Blanco said.

'I've felt better,' said Amy.

'Are we going to suffocate as he said?' Quinn asked.

'No,' Rorschach said. 'We know the *Hermes* doesn't have any torpedoes, so they can't hit us under the water.' He spun the periscope and peered into it. 'And they're already sailing away. North, to Canada. That's my best guess.'

'Can we fix the *Seawolf*?' Amy asked.

Rorschach nodded. 'We've already stopped some of the water coming in, so yes, I think she'll be all right. But we can't sustain any more damage. All she can do is limp back to the harbour in Canada. That's it.'

'Damn it all!' Hunter said. 'We lost the idol and Hanna. The Illuminati have seen four of the five idols and the Creed have got all five of them. No prizes for guessing who's going to be last to discover de Gama's big secret.'

'Take it easy, Max,' Amy said. 'As soon as we fix the radio, we can call the chopper back out to us. We'll be in Halifax in a few hours. It's not much of a head start, plus Hanna might slow them down.'

'Not if she has any sense,' Hunter said. 'She needs to look after herself and give them what they want. In the meantime, we need to try to work out the idol's message using her translation work on the other four relics. Maybe we stand a chance.'

'And how are we going to do that, without the idol?' Quinn asked.

Amy waved her phone. 'I got a picture of it.'

Blanco shrugged. 'Then let's get on with it. Time is running out fast.'

34

As the *Seawolf* limped back to Canada, a long, quiet meal in the galley provided the time they needed to examine the symbols on the idol recently liberated from the rusting wreckage so far below them. In the hour it had taken for them to fix the radio and get the chopper out to their location, Hunter had made good progress. Using Hanna's translation of the other relics, the carving on the idol had given up its secret in less time than he had thought.

'"...Third, Then Go to Where they Became Snakes."'

Amy listened carefully to Hunter as he spoke the words on the idol. De Gama had carved the original verse in Spanish, but its translation was a simple matter of typing it into a search engine. Now they had their final clue, everything was falling into place.

'Does this make things clearer, Max?' Blanco asked hopefully.

Hunter swallowed a sip of beer and took a bite out of a large hamburger. Nodding in full appreciation at the perfect blend of beef, salad, and pickles, he swallowed this too and gave the chef over behind the counter a large smile and a thumbs up.

'Bloody amazing, Chef!'

'Thanks.'

Amy kept her frustration in check. 'Max, I know Oskar Rorschach lays on a great meal, I truly do, but I think we should probably turn our attention to the golden idol we nearly just died salvaging from the *Titanic*, don't you? Hanna's life may depend on it!'

'Of course, and Hanna will be fine. She's of too much value to Brodie right up until she leads them to whatever the big mystery is. We'll have got her back to safety by then. Count on it.'

Jodie tossed him a napkin. 'You have some tomato ketchup on your mouth, and your chin, and your shirt.'

'Oh, thanks.' He dabbed at the slopped ketchup without embarrassment. 'That only happens with the very best burgers. Don't worry, it's a good sign.'

'I'm very pleased for you,' Amy said, 'but again, getting back to the idol...'

'Oh yeah, sure,' he said, setting the half-eaten burger down and picking up a picture of the idol. 'A thing of rare and exquisite beauty, to be sure, and without a doubt, an authentic piece of Muisca goldsmithing. It's pretty obvious which order to put the clues in. The ring is the first verse: "First, Welcome to the Quest of a Lifetime." Then, the compass has the second clue: "Second, You must find the Good Woman and Her Man." Then, the idol: "Third, Then go to Where they Became Snakes." Then the chalice: "Fourth, From here March one Milla at Two Hundred and Eighty Degrees."'

'A milla?' Quinn asked.

Hunter smiled. 'A milla is four and half thousand feet, by the way, an old Spanish mile. Finally, we have the crucifix: "Fifth, in the House of the Sun is the Garden of the Golden One – there, See what is Unseeable and the Treasure is Yours."'

'And what does this add up to?' asked Jodie. 'I mean, it's great that we translated them all, but they're still pretty cryptic. What do they actually mean?'

'I'm glad you asked,' Hunter said with a grin. 'Because I can help you with that. I already know that the Good Woman refers to Bachué, the Muisca Mother Goddess sometimes called Furachogua in the Chibcha language.'

'Wait,' Quinn said. 'Is this you or Google?'

'Me. I went to Oxford, darling.'

She rolled her eyes. 'I wish I never asked.'

'Keep going,' Amy said, clearly impressed.

'So, we know it's the quest of a lifetime,' Hunter said. 'De Gama tells us that on the ring. We also know we need to go to Muisca territory, which the Spanish conquered in 1537, from the reference to Bachué on the compass. After this, he tells us on the idol to go to where Bachué and the man, with whom she gave birth to the world, became snakes. We know that Bachué was delivered from the Underworld through Lake Iguaque to give birth to the entire human race. We also know this is where she and her man became snakes after they had created humanity, and vanished back into the Underworld. This lake is in the Colombian Highlands, up in the Andes. After this, de Gama leaves our penultimate clue on the chalice, which is to walk one milla at two-eighty degrees from the lake. I think when we do this, X will mark the spot.'

'WTF, Hunter,' said Quinn, pulling her hoodie over her head. 'That's insane.'

'But even I'm impressed,' Jodie said.

'I absolutely live for that,' said Hunter.

'I try and say something nice...'

Hunter laughed. 'Kidding. Just kidding.'

'Wait,' Blanco said. 'Aren't we all forgetting about the last clue on the crucifix? The part that says...' He leaned over and looked at Hanna's notes. '"Fifth, See what is Unseeable and the Treasure is Yours." That sounds pretty weird.'

'Yeah, I couldn't do anything with that bit,' Hunter said, scratching his head.

'I say we just get there and work it out when we're on-site,' Lewis said.

Blanco stretched his arms and yawned. 'Interesting stuff, Max, but I'm getting too old for all this action. Maybe I'll feel better after a short nap.'

'You can sleep on the chopper,' Amy said, gently kicking his foot and making him open his eyes. 'And after that, you can sleep on the plane to Colombia. And you should get all the sleep you can because something tells me we might not get another chance to sleep for a long time when we land.'

35

An endless blue sky stretched over a rugged landscape of lush equatorial jungles and mountains carpeted with verdant rainforests. The midday sun pitched down and illuminated everything in a dazzling, white-hot glare. Hunter took it all in as the plane descended towards the runway. When it landed, he was first off the aircraft, excited to relive some of the good old days spent exploring the wildest parts of the world.

Amy processed the team through customs and one of the officials showed them to a private area where two well-equipped Jeeps were awaiting them. One was for them, and the other was surrounded by Delta Force soldiers, just as Jim Gates had guaranteed before they left Halifax. There were four of them, as expected, and they were all smoking and talking quietly among themselves. Used to working on extremely classified projects, the men introduced themselves without handshakes or humour as Nixon, Carter, Reagan, and Bush. Hunter, who had worked with British SAS, understood their reluctance to give their real names.

The Delta team climbed into their Jeep and fired it up.

'Looks like we're off,' Hunter said, climbing up into their own Jeep.

Jodie and the others followed him into the vehicle. They were all glad to be out of the sun and inside the nice air-conditioned interior of the Jeep. Jodie commented how they needed to make up some time and got her iPhone out to check in with Gates.

They soon left the sprawling city behind and drove up into the mountains they had seen from the aircraft on their way into the country. The mountains here were not high enough for snow, but the peaks were scrubby and rocky where the altitude was too high for the rainforest to grow. They turned off the main road and followed Quinn's GPS guidance into a warren of narrow roads that became lanes which became unsealed tracks. Dust churned up in the air behind them.

Two hours after the airport, Quinn said they needed to leave the track they were on and turn off into a large, sloping field. They pulled in, followed by the Delta team. When the Jeeps' engines were switched off, they opened their doors and stepped outside. The field was surrounded by thick, tropical undergrowth, and looming up at the far end, blocking their view of the sky almost entirely, was one of the foothills leading up to the highlands beyond.

Hunter breathed deeply and took it all in. A gentle breeze was blowing over the jungle canopy below them and washing over the field. It felt good, rippling their clothes and hair and cooling the sweat on their bodies. The readout on the Jeep's dash had said the temperature was already thirty-five degrees Celsius and humidity at 70 per cent. It would get easier as they moved up into the highlands.

'The trail's up there,' Blanco said, pointing. He'd been having a quiet conversation with a couple of the Delta force guys. Now, they wandered slowly back to the rest of the team. 'It looks pretty safe from here, but I guess it'll get a lot tougher as we go higher.'

They got their packs and weapons from the back of the Jeeps and after moving the Jeeps out of sight and into the shade of the surrounding trees, they began to ascend the trail. At first, they were flanked by thick jungle on both sides. This went on for several miles and around an hour of trekking until it began to thin out slightly with the altitude.

They took a break an hour later on the banks of a rushing river. It tumbled down the mountain, carving its way through the undergrowth as it had done for millennia. The peaceful, tranquil, and beautiful nature of the place was lost on no one. This was as untouched as nature got, and for a moment, it was almost possible to forget why they were here. Francisco de Gama's mysterious Golden One. The exotic call of some tropical birds startled them from their reverie, and they picked up their packs, took some water, and made off once again up the track.

They continued to ascend towards the next waypoint for another hour but then were all surprised when Quinn told them to stop and leave the track. Here, she explained, was the best place to head into the jungle and began the final trek to their destination.

'Is the kid sure?' Nixon asked Jodie. He was standing right next to Quinn.

'I'm sure,' the young goth said, unfazed by his attitude.

'I sure hope she's sure,' Reagan said.

'Yeah,' Carter added, 'because I'm not sure she's sure about how sure she is.'

Jodie grinned. 'Okay, I see. You're having some fun.'

'Not much,' Bush said, but with a grin. He checked his watch. 'Nightfall in less than an hour. We need to make tracks.'

'Wait,' Jodie said. 'If this is the best place to access the lost city, why are there no tracks? We know Bauer and the Creed left the *Titanic* site well before us, and with all the knowledge they needed to find their way here. Something's not right.'

'Maybe they couldn't work it out,' Lewis said.

'I don't know about that,' said Jodie, still looking unhappy. 'They worked out everything else, and now they have Hanna, too. If she's still alive.'

'She's still alive, kid,' Blanco said. 'Thinking anything else is just letting her down.'

As the sun sank beneath the jungle canopy arching above the trail, the sky changed from blue to orange to violet to star-studded black with the usual speed of this part of the world. No dawdling twilights here, just a speedy, no-nonsense transition from day to night in the blink of an eye. And not much temperature change either, Quinn noted with dismay.

'How much farther?' Jodie said.

'Right up ahead,' said Hunter. 'And stop whining.'

'I'm not whining, I'm tired. There's a difference. It's about a million degrees and it's so humid it feels like we're marching through warm honey.'

Some of the Delta soldiers laughed. Nixon said, 'I hear that.'

Hunter studied the paper map they had made with de Gama's coordinates and traced some of the contour lines with his finger. 'It really should be dead ahead of us. I don't understand.'

Blanco stepped forward and pulled his machete out of a sheath on his belt. It came out with a metallic scraping noise and glinted in the moonlight. He walked into the trees ahead of them and they heard him hacking and grunting in the dark.

Hunter followed him into the trees and drew his machete too, joining in and helping his old friend as they tried to make headway through the thick undergrowth. Vines and creepers clung to them as they hacked and chopped. Then, Lewis and the Delta guys were alongside them, helping with the struggle.

'You find anything?' Amy asked.

'Not yet,' Reagan called out. 'All I got so far is some blisters.'

With each metre that gave nothing but hard work, Hunter felt the same frustration as everyone else on the team. All of this was taking valuable time, and nobody knew where the Creed was, or what had happened to Hanna. The ticking clock was no man's friend, at least not tonight. Not here. Then, in the darkness, the tip of his machete struck something solid.

36

'Wait! I hit some stone.'

Everyone stopped hacking at the plants and stared at him.

'Where?' Lewis asked.

'Right here,' he said, gently tugging some vines and other plants away from a space right in front of his face. 'Torch, please.'

'Flashlight,' Jodie said.

Blanco smiled. Like everyone else, he was relieved they were finally making some progress. 'Either will do.'

Carter handed Hunter his torch, and he clicked it on and held it shoulder height, peering at the stone surface he had struck moments earlier. He blinked in the sweaty night, surprised by what he was seeing. He turned to Amy, who was now standing right behind them with Jodie and Quinn beside her.

'It's Muisca, all right. There's an excellent carving of their sun god on it.'

'Then we found it,' Jodie said. 'About goddamn time.'

Hunter, who was slightly further ahead of the others, turned to Bush, who was the furthest away from him, and said, 'How far does it go along?'

The Delta soldier moved forward through the undergrowth, hacking another metre or so away until they all heard the clash of steel on stone. 'At least to here.'

'Must be the city wall de Gama wrote about,' Lewis said in wonder.

Quinn said, 'Wait, didn't he say it went all the way around the city?'

Lewis nodded. 'He sure did. Either we find some kind of gateway or arch or something, or we have to go over it or under it.'

Hunter took a step back and tried to see the top of the wall, but his view was quickly obscured by dense tangles of tropical plants. 'That's helpful. And de Gama never said how high the walls went anyway.'

'So, we go under?' Quinn said.

'Not without a few days, some explosives and shovels and a few hundred litres of water,' said Hunter. 'It's a gate or we go over the top. That means climbing up these vines and hacking our way up, every foot we go. Hard, hard work, but easier than digging.'

Jodie reached out and ran her hands up against the rough stone wall. 'I'm liking an archway better.'

'Which could be hundreds of metres in either direction,' Hunter said. 'And that means hacking our way through a hell of a lot more undergrowth than we've just done right now. Could take hours, could take days. I'm recommending over the top. We know there's a natural limit to how high they could build it, right? If we can just get through some of this jungle and see the top of the wall, we can fire up a grappling hook and the rest is as easy as apple pie.'

Blanco agreed immediately. So did everyone else.

Hunter was first up the vines. Pulling himself up as he had trained on ropes so many times in the army, he found his recent lack of exercise combined with his slight weight gain had conspired against him. Working much harder than he had expected, he slowly climbed up to around ten feet, looped his left arm and feet in the vine, and started hacking at the jungle canopy. The work was hard, and after ten minutes he climbed back down and Reagan went up to carry on his work.

Then Nixon.

Then Carter.

Then Bush.

After several hours of hard labour, dawn was slowly rising in the east. Lewis was up at a height of forty feet, hacking away at giant leaves and creepers, when suddenly he cried out to everyone standing below him on the forest floor. Everyone shared a glance, half concerned, half excited.

'You all right, Ben?' Hunter called up.

'You bet! We did it! We got through the canopy. I can see the top of the wall.'

'How much higher?' Blanco said.

'We're already there! I'm level with it. My God! You should see what's on the other side!'

'I'm going to fire up a grappling hook, Ben,' Nixon said. 'It's going to park its ass a few yards to your left, so watch yourself.'

'Got it.'

They climbed over the wall and slowly found their way safely back down the other side. They found themselves in an overgrown labyrinth of ancient houses and temples and streets. Narrow alleys, blocked by dense tangles of vines and creepers, stretched away on both sides of them as they walked further into the heart of the ancient lost city.

The farther they walked, the more concerned Amy grew. Ahead of her, Lewis and Jodie were trotting up an embankment and sweeping flashlights over the ruined buildings. Behind her, Hunter was strangely agitated, referring to his notes with his flashlight and mumbling something about the inner temple.

'What's up, Max?' she asked.

He looked through the manuscript. 'I think we have another challenge up ahead. Some kind of temple de Gama calls the House of the Sun. He says the Garden of the Golden One is inside it, but unseeable, remember.'

'What the hell does that mean?' Jodie asked, turning.

Blanco was over to their right. 'I think we got your temple, Max. Problem is, we're not first.'

Everyone looked at him.

Amy's concern grew. 'Sal?'

'Bauer and McCabe,' he said. 'They're down in front of a large pyramid over to the west.'

Hunter climbed up onto the ruins beside Blanco. 'Yeah, that's the place. That's the House of the Sun. Looks like Hanna's still all right. For now, at least.'

'Then what do we do?' asked Quinn. 'This place gives me the serious creeps. I just want to get out as fast as possible.'

'No one's going anywhere until we save Hanna,' Amy said.

Hunter clambered down from a broken wall and dusted his hands off on his trousers. 'And find the Golden One.'

'So, what next?' Lewis asked.

'They're putting explosives around the temple's main entrance,' Blanco said. 'I say we wait here and have some water and let those assholes do the heavy lifting.'

'Good plan,' Hunter said. 'When they blow the door, we can go right in behind them.'

37

Down in the heart of the ancient city, Bauer watched as the small army at his command finished placing explosives on the temple wall and backed away to a safe distance, awaiting his order to detonate them. The day had dawned but a thick, humid mist was still clinging to anything it touched. 'This is an auspicious moment for the Creed,' he said proudly to McCabe. 'And you have played an important part in it. You will be rewarded for your loyalty.'

Hanna sat on a nearby rock, hands tied securely behind her back. The cloth gag that had been in her mouth was now hanging around her neck, removed by one of Bauer's men to let her sip from a canteen. Now she gave a sad laugh.

Bauer turned to her. 'You have something to add to our conversation?'

'The only rewards any of you guys are getting are going to be in hell.'

The men around her laughed. Posch walked over to her and started to put the gag back in her mouth, but Bauer stopped him.

'No, leave her! I want to hear what she has to say.'

The ex-commando tugged the cloth back out of her mouth with an aggressive yank and scowled at her before walking away.

'I don't think any of you want to hear what I have to say,' Hanna said, anger rising inside her.

'Then shut up,' McCabe said. 'And let us get on with our work.'

She scoffed. 'Work! Plundering and pillaging ancient archaeological sites for the worst possible reasons. No wonder Max thinks you're such an asshole, not to mention a pathetic little thief.'

'Max Hunter is an arrogant bastard,' McCabe said, giving her a greasy grin. 'And a dead man walking. Next time I see him, I'll put a bullet through his brain, personally.'

Hanna wanted to speak but felt the words dry up in her mouth. McCabe seemed to exude evil. It was like it radiated away from him in an aura. She didn't want to hear anything else he had to say.

'There!' Bauer said triumphantly. 'This must be the archway we're looking for. De Gama describes it perfectly in his memoirs.' He dropped his voice to a whisper full of awe as he spoke from memory. 'It was concealing some kind of tunnel. Let's go. We're almost there.'

The tunnel was now almost clear enough for them to walk into. After the men had pulled away the last remaining vines and creepers, Bauer stepped through the Sun God arch and entered the tunnel. He shone a flashlight down into the dusty gloom and sniffed.

'Is that a light I see?'

'I think it is.'

'How is there a light coming from inside a temple?'

'It's not inside, it's leading to a garden.'

* * *

'You think there's another way in?' Jodie asked, watching as the Bauer party disappeared into the temple.

Hunter shrugged. 'I don't know, but I doubt it. Even if there were, it would be in the same condition as the one we just watched those arseholes break into. Vines, creepers, boulders – you name it. Even if we could find it in the first place, it would take us even longer to make it accessible because even with the Delta guys, we have a tiny fraction of Bauer's manpower.'

'So what do we do?' Quinn said, slapping at a mosquito.

Hunter said, 'We wait until the main force is inside, take out those two guards left up top, and then we go in after them. Sound good?'

'Sounds good to me,' Lewis said. 'That way we know we've got our backs covered before we go in.'

Reagan and Nixon agreed. Blanco nodded silently. He was already checking his weapons. Now he aimed his gun at one of Bauer's two guards outside the Temple of the Sun. 'Just say when, Amy.'

'When.'

He fired. The gun kicked back in his hand and a puff of smoke drifted into the air. The man on the wall tumbled down silently, a bullet through his brain. The other man whirled around and crouched down, sweeping his gun in an arc as he searched for whoever had killed his associate. He stood no chance. Blanco fired a second shot and sent him over the temple wall to meet his dead friend.

'You still got it, Sal,' Amy said.

'Now we move,' Blanco said. 'Before something happens to Hanna.'

* * *

Bauer was almost beside himself with excitement as he led his force along the tunnel and into the garden. Beside him, Hackl held the flashlight in one hand and a freshly oiled Mauser in the other. McCabe and Posch followed, also gripping flashlights and handguns. At the back, Zeller was a step behind Hanna, pushing the muzzle of his handgun in the small of her back and forcing her forwards against her will.

'I see steps,' McCabe said. 'Dead ahead.'

When he saw them, Bauer's eyes lit up like shop windows. 'Could they be...?'

'The Steps of Bachué,' he said, moving forward.

'Is this the right way into the garden?' Bauer asked. 'What about that way, through the arch with those symbols?'

Hackl shrugged. Beside him, an agitated McCabe pushed Hanna Vikander a step closer to Bauer. 'Ask her,' he said. 'She knows.'

'Well,' Bauer said, reaching out and grabbing a fistful of her hair. Yanking her head back, he leaned in close to her and said, 'What do those symbols mean?'

Hanna read them carefully. 'They say the Steps of Bachué are a trap.'

'She's lying!' Posch said. 'Shoot her!'

'I'm not lying. That is what they say.'

Posch sneered. 'In that case, you won't mind showing us how safe the archway is.'

Bauer released her hair. 'No, she's too valuable. I need a man to volunteer.'

Hackl immediately spat on the ground and raised his hand. 'Me.'

'Good man.'

They watched in silence as the giant padded through the archway unharmed. A few steps later he stopped and turned. He shrugged. 'I think we're good to go.'

'Then let's move out,' Bauer said. 'HARPA is on our tail, and the absence of the Illuminati is making me more nervous than their presence.'

* * *

Hunter and Amy led the team along the same path recently used by Bauer and his group, cautiously following their footprints as they made their way into the heart of the temple. They reached the final chamber to find a small space hewn from the bedrock. Carved into the walls were crude images of Muisca deities. Hunter tried to push the stone but was unable to manage it on his own. He looked over at Lewis, but the young ex-marine was already walking up the slope towards him. When they reached the stone archway, Hunter pulled up to a stop.

'Which way do we go?' Quinn asked.

'This way,' Lewis said, following the footprints towards the arch.

'No, wait.' Hunter was staring at the symbols above the two arches. 'They went the wrong way. I'm only just starting to understand these letters, but thanks to Hanna's notes I can say they're heading towards some kind of religious room, a place for worship. I think it's called the devotional room. She wouldn't have made a mistake like that. She's taking them on a wild goose chase and giving us time to reach the Golden One first. We need to go this way, up these steps.'

'Wait,' Amy said. 'That carving there looks like one of the Atlantean weapons we saw up in Greenland.'

'How the hell is that possible?' Lewis asked.

Hunter ran his hands over the carving. It wasn't identical to those he had seen in the Arctic Circle, but it bore an uncanny resemblance.

'I think this is a question for later. We need to keep moving.'

They climbed the steps. At the top, they were bathed in the warm, golden glow of the rising sun. Ahead of them was a vast, overgrown garden full of sculptures and statues and pathways and stone benches. All of it was covered in a mass of vines and creepers and exotic flowers, except for the pathways. A paradise garden more beautiful than any of them had seen before.

'Odd,' Hunter said.

'Yeah,' said Amy. 'Who's doing the gardening?'

Tipped up against the wall beside them was an old, battered Roman scutum. Blanco poked at the dented shield with his boot. 'Why would there be a Roman shield here?'

Lewis scratched his jaw, as puzzled as the rest of the team. 'Good question.'

'And an Egyptian amulet,' Amy said, reaching down into the grass and picking up a small piece of gold jewellery. She turned to Hunter, handing it to him. 'That is what this is, right?'

He smiled at her. 'I'm impressed, but also sort of freaked out, frankly. According to our best historical accounts – to *all* historical accounts – this entire region wasn't discovered by European cultures until the sixteenth century. By people like Francisco de Gama.'

'Maybe he brought them here. It's still weird though.'

Hunter turned. 'Don't you remember our conversation with Julian Walters during the Atlantis mission, and how we talked about Egyptian artifacts from a thousand years before the time of Christ somehow wound up in El Salvador? The conclusion was obvious – Atlantis. Only a civilisation as powerful as Atlantis could have delivered those relics to that jungle, and if you ask me, this is the same thing going on right here, right now. Whatever the Golden One truly is, I'd bet my career on it being originally from Atlantis. Same goes for the stories of Viracocha's thunderbolts – maybe they were Atlantean spears. Only a trade network as vast and far-reaching as Atlantis's could bring these ancient weapons and technology so far.'

'And I think I see the Golden One,' Quinn said. 'Over there inside that walled garden just in front of that weird pyramid.'

Hunter looked and saw a fountain in the centre of an ornamental garden. 'A garden within a garden. You all wait here, and keep an eye out for Bauer.'

He went up on his own, determined that if there were any other nasty surprises, he'd be the only victim. As it happened, it was safe, and he found himself staring down into what looked almost like molten gold. But there was no heat, no smoke, no steam. Whatever it was, it was quite cool. The exhaustion he felt from this brutal mission seemed to fade away as he stared down at it. Not magic, because he hadn't even touched it yet, but awe and shock. Or was it something more? He called the others up to join him.

'What is it?' Quinn asked.

'It's eternal life,' Hunter said. 'The Golden One is the elixir in this fountain. See how it shimmers? Feel how much stronger and younger you feel?'

'I can't believe this is real,' Jodie said. 'It's like something out of a movie.'

Hunter was also struggling to accept what he was seeing. 'It's real all right, but I can barely believe it, either.'

'Are we sure it's real though?' Amy said. 'I mean, maybe it's some kind of trick the ancients played on anyone stupid enough to believe it. Or maybe De Gama set it all up as some kind of joke.'

Blanco whistled as he took in the incredible fountain. 'Yeah, but no. This is no joke. This is really it. We found the Fountain of Youth.'

'And before Bauer and McCabe, too,' Lewis said. 'Which is kinda funny.'

The sound of gunshots and screaming outside the garden echoed over the towering wall. 'I don't think they find it quite as funny as you do,' Amy said.

'I guess not.'

Hunter stepped forward and stared into the water. Its smooth, golden surface reflected his face like a mirror. It looked less like water than a pool of golden mercury, rippling here and there as the water from the top of the fountain tumbled down over the tiers and splashed into the circular reservoir at the base. 'El Dorado,' he mumbled. 'The Golden One... It wasn't a reference to a god or goddess, or even the city itself, but to this fountain. To the water of life.'

The rest of the team took a step forward and joined him, each momentarily forgetting about the threat outside as their attention was stolen by the mesmerising shimmer of the golden elixir.

'Anyone going to try some?' Quinn said.

'What about you?' said Jodie.

'I don't think so.'

After a pause, Blanco said, 'Wait. Why can't this place be seen from the air? I just don't understand it. It's pretty big and obviously manmade. It would be on Google Earth or something, for sure.'

'I think I know,' Amy said. 'Hand me your flashlight.'

She took hold of his Maglite and shone the beam over the fountain. The dawn was still just dark enough for them to see what she had guessed might happen, and it shocked them all. The beam shone straight all the way to the fountain, but then bent around unnaturally to the right, hitting the garden's north wall. When she tried to move the beam back over to illuminate another part of the fountain by sweeping it over to the left, the beam slid over the top again and shot around to the left. None of them had ever seen anything like it in their lives.

'What the hell's going on?' Jodie asked, shocked.

'The water has some kind of light-bending property,' Hunter said. 'Whatever is giving it its powers clearly has some kind of effect on gravity. Weird.'

'Yeah,' Quinn said. 'Weird. Also, scary. If that stuff can bend light, what the hell is it going to do to your insides if you drink it?'

'Just what I was thinking,' Lewis said.

'Whatever it is,' Amy said, 'Hunter's right. It must have something to do with its life-giving powers.'

Blanco looked up at the sky and then back down to the fountain. 'Now we know why no one has ever found it until now.'

'And why the sneaky old bastard de Gama told us it was unseeable,' Jodie said. 'See the unseeable...'

Their conversation was broken by the sound of men's boots on gravel. They turned to see Hans Bauer and his small army filing into the garden. Hackl was gripping Hanna Vikander. One of her eyes was black and her lip was split and bleeding.

Bauer beamed. 'Ah, Dr Hunter and Agent Fox. How good to see you again. On behalf of the Creed, allow me to extend my apologies for what must now happen to you. Drop your guns. You are outgunned and outmanned. This is over for you. The Golden One is now in the possession of the Creed.'

'We can't let a power like this get into your hands,' Amy said.

Bauer laughed. 'The Golden One, the elixir sparkling in this fountain, is the water of life. For us, it means eternal life. This is much more valuable than mere gold. After all, what is all the gold in the world when you are dead and underground?'

'He makes a good point,' Hunter said.

'Silence!' Bauer yelled. 'Take their weapons, McCabe! Then line them up against that wall and shoot them dead. Every last one of them.'

'Sir.'

McCabe obeyed his orders, stripping the team of their weapons and forcing them to stand in front of the inner wall in front of the pyramid Quinn had first seen, hands on their heads. When they were in a line, Hackl forced Hanna over beside Hunter. 'You die too,' he said and slapped her face.

Hunter bristled but calmed down fast when Posch swung a carbine in his face.

'It's time for you to die now,' Bauer said. A deep peal of thunder roared in the sky and heavy rain began to pour down. Bauer raised his voice. 'And at the end of your lives, you learned that no one ever beats the Creed! As we escape on our transport plane your corpses will rot in the jungle as nothing more than maggot food. Hackl, Zeller... Fire!'

The sound of heavy machinegun fire punched the steamy dawn like nails hammered into a coffin.

38

When Hunter heard the deathly report of the guns, he thought he was dead. When he knew he wasn't dead, he figured something must have gone wrong. Not for him, but for Bauer. He opened an eye and saw Bauer's men fleeing for their lives. Behind him, he heard the noise of more machinegun fire and saw chunky rounds from what he guessed was a chain gun blasting into the ground, nipping at the Creed's fleeing heels. Then, a chopper ripped over their heads, almost low enough to touch.

'We need to split,' he called out. 'Head for the pyramid behind the garden.'

His friends were already on it. They reached the garden and ran up the stone staircase leading up to the fountain. Rounding the enormous silver reservoir, they made their way over to the pyramid, knowing the only way out of here would be to fight the Creed to the death.

Hunter was the first to reach the bottom of the pyramid. It loomed above them, its highest tiers an ornate study of carved cornices and gargoyles stretching high into the sky above the garden. He leaped up the first few stone steps and turned around, looking back over the top of the team and down the slope towards where the garden's main entrance was located. 'They're regrouping, but still pinned down by fire from the chopper!'

'They'll be here,' Amy called back. 'And when they are, we have to fight.'

The Creed piled in through the giant stone archway at the far end of the garden, guns at the ready. In the middle of them, Hunter saw Bauer screaming at Hackl and Posch to go back and secure some of the elixir. 'Secure some at all costs!' As the chopper turned in the sky to make another attack, Bauer ordered the rest of his men to kill Team HARPA.

His men charged forward, guns blazing in the dawn. Their rounds shredded the thick, tropical undergrowth and pinged off the stone walls. They screamed with rage as they advanced into the garden, taking cover here and there behind the vine-covered statues, benches, and pillars.

The rest of the HARPA team had now joined Hunter up at the pyramid and they were all making their way around to the rear to find some cover of their own. Blanco turned and fired on one of the men at the Creed's frontline, his shot echoing loudly in the densely overgrown garden. The man dropped his gun, cried out, and clutched his stomach. Blanco's next shot dropped him like a rock.

Lewis fired almost immediately after Blanco, also striking another Creed man. This time, the first shot was the lethal one, blasting one side of the man's skull clean off and sending him spinning back over one of the stone benches. A dozen terrified parrots in the tree above the bench screeched and flapped away over the southern wall and disappeared.

'Wish we could do that!' Quinn said.

Hunter fired, striking one of the men in the chest and killing him instantly, but it wasn't enough to deter the others from making the base of the pyramid and starting to climb up after them. He ordered the team to fire on the attackers, and they unleashed the biggest firestorm they could. Some bullets found their targets and killed Creed soldiers as they stormed the pyramid; others missed and ricocheted off the stonework into the dawn. It wasn't enough. Even with the chopper attacking them and forcing them to fight on two fronts, Bauer's Creed forces were a small army. Well-armed, well-trained, and thirsty for blood.

And the mystical power of the ancient fountain and its golden elixir.

Hunter led the HARPA team around to the far side of the temple. Almost at the very top now, they had a perfect view of the entire garden and the wild jungle beyond its high stone walls. The vista was breathtaking as the sun rose from the eastern horizon, but the area's beauty was stained by the thought of it being their final resting place.

Below them, Hunter watched Bauer and his most loyal men swarming around the fountain. The chopper had made another pass and was rotating around for a third strike. He fired on them, driving them back behind a circle of carved pillars. Blanco and Jodie fired next, backing him up. Amy and Lewis stood to each side, covering them. Sitting on a stone step slightly below them, Quinn was desperately trying to reach help on the radio but getting nothing but static in response. They were just too remote.

'Still nothing,' she called out.

'And we're running out of time,' Hunter said. 'The Creed is halfway up the pyramid and Bauer is back at the fountain. We can't keep this up for much longer.' New attackers streamed through the gate at the end of the garden, adding yet again to Bauer's forces. 'We need to retreat.'

'But to where?' Jodie asked. 'We're cornered. We can't get inside the temple and that's a dead end anyway. As for running back down behind the temple, there are just more overgrown pathways and then the stone wall. We're trapped, Hunter.'

Creed streamed all over the pyramid like ants. They were at the top now, closing in on the HARPA team and heavily outgunning them, mostly with compact machine pistols but also some grenades. One of them now selected a grenade and hurled it over the top of the temple. It landed with a hard metallic smack on the stone step beside Quinn.

She screamed and panicked, tumbling over and dropping the two-way radio. As the radio clattered all the way to the bottom of the temple and vanished into a knot of vines, Lewis scrambled over and snatched up the grenade and threw it back over the pyramid capstone as hard as he could. Quinn was still trembling when it dropped out of sight behind them and detonated. They all heard a deep, bass roar and a flash of bright light. Body parts and jets of blood sprayed up into the air, mixing with the smoke. Men screamed in agony.

'I see a plane!' Lewis yelled. 'Circling high above.'

Hunter looked up and saw it, barely visible in the storm clouds.

'Looks like it's the Creed's long-range transport that Bauer bragged to us about,' Blanco said. 'A Spartan. They must have cleared a landing strip somewhere ready to airlift the fountain out of the jungle.'

The plane gradually began to descend.

'Not on my watch,' Hunter said. 'Lewis, do we still have the grenade launcher?'

'We sure do.'

As Lewis pulled the launcher from his pack, Hunter tracked the transport plane across the snowy sky. It was not hard to miss. The C-27J Spartan was a beast of an aircraft. Airframe twenty-two metres long and nearly ten metres high and over thirty-thousand kilos in weight.

The chunky plane was used as a tactical airlift for various operations ranging from humanitarian relief missions in the remotest places on Earth to transporting soldiers into places with unsurfaced airstrips. It was a big plane and easy for Hunter to keep an eye on as it lumbered its way around to the unseen landing strip hiding somewhere in the jungle.

But soon the electrical storm would swallow it up, so Hunter knew his time was limited. Bringing the grenade launcher up onto his shoulder, he continued to track the plane from right to left. Rain blowing all over the place obscured his vision and the wind buffeted him, knocking him off aim. He slowed his breathing and aimed again. This time, he was faster. Just as the Spartan was vanishing into the clouds, he squeezed the trigger and unleashed hell.

The launcher gave a solid kick and then the grenade was loose, ripping through the rainstorm at the head of a twisting column of white smoke. The storm soon whipped the exhaust smoke away into nothing, but Hunter had aimed ahead of the plane and considered the windspeed before firing. Seconds later, the grenade hit the plane's tail and it blew up in a grotesque fireball that scratched the sky with a burning light and heat. Hunter shielded his eyes as the plane fell from the sky in a cloud of flames and black smoke. It went down like he knew it would – fast and hard. There was no controlling a thirty-thousand-kilo transport plane after its tail was blown clear off.

When it hit the ground, it shook the jungle like an earthquake and nearly knocked him off his feet. He regained his balance just as the wrecked aircraft exploded in a second fireball. He had also expected this –

the crash into the ground had broken the wings up and spilled the kerosene all over the place. Fire from the original grenade explosion had ignited the highly flammable fuel and consumed the rest of the plane in a tremendous burning inferno.

With the sound of the explosion still echoing over the jungle, birds raced away from the scene in terror. Hunter was watching the chaos, waiting for the smoke to clear. When it did, he saw the front of the aircraft had broken away from the rest of the plane on impact and was relatively intact, untouched by the explosions at the tail and the mid-section.

Now, he watched in the distance as men poured out of the Spartan's wrecked nose, smoke bubbling out of the windows around them. Some jumped from the severed section behind the cockpit, others climbed out of the smashed windows at the front. He counted five, then six, seven. Maybe more, but it was hard to tell in the mayhem and the heat from the fire was scorching the surrounding jungle canopy. Before any could get away from the burning carcass, the chopper swooped down and cut them all to pieces. Then the aircraft turned and headed back to the hidden garden.

'Good work, Max,' Amy said. 'Good work, but we still have the chopper to deal with!'

Her words were followed by a brutal slaughter. No sooner had she finished talking, the chopper roared down low and opened fire on the garden. Spitting fire from its chin-mounted death maker, the helicopter fired on the Creed and took out Zeller, Hackl, and Posch in one brutal burst of bullets fired from just above their heads.

Bauer and McCabe sprinted away from their dead colleagues, trying to make their way back down the garden and into the Temple of the Sun, desperate for cover. It was too late. Hunter watched without emotion as the helicopter's heavy-duty chain gun cut them in half, sending their severed bloody bodies crashing into the earth.

'My God,' he muttered, barely able to register what he had just witnessed. Just like that, in a heartbeat, the Creed's senior echelon had been murdered, and his old nemesis Brodie McCabe was among the body count.

'Bastard got what he deserved,' Jodie said.

Hunter shook his head, still in shock. 'No one deserves that.'

Still frozen with disbelief, they were all caught off guard when the chopper rotated in the steamy air and landed down by the temple. Half a dozen heavily armed men leaped out and began firing on them as the chopper took off once again.

'Looks like the chain gun ran out,' Blanco said. 'We need some cover. Now.'

39

The HARPA team sprinted towards the temple, exhausted but forced to fight all over again. This time, a new enemy.

Illuminati.

The Disciples gave no quarter. The HARPA team was small, isolated, cornered, and running out of ammunition. Razquin, the Illuminati leader, could have offered their lives in return for surrender, but instead, he ordered yet another wave forward to kill them all.

Hunter gripped his gun, freshly reloaded with his last magazine, and charged forward into the fray. He trusted his team to retreat and leave him on his own if it came to it. In a brutal exchange of fire with the leading Illuminati soldiers, he rapidly emptied his magazine, taking out all but three. The other men were also out of bullets. He now reached for the combat knife swinging from his belt. They did the same and rushed him with their blades glinting in the rising sun.

Their assault was vicious, slashing and stabbing at him with their knives like the deranged cult members they truly were. He thought he was a dead man and called out to Amy to retreat and lead the team back to the relative safety of the garden's western end. As one of them lunged at him, he ducked and then sprang across the path and struck him in the face with the grip of his knife. The blow was poorly timed but hard, and knocked the stunned man back into a thick tangle of vines behind him. He cracked his head on a stone and died instantly, but the others kept coming.

A blade whistled past his face, millimetres from his cheek, and he flicked his head back to miss it. The move was good, missing the blade's razor-sharp tip but also driving the back of his head unexpectedly into the face of a man he didn't even know was behind him.

The man cried out in pain as his nose broke, snapped, and collapsed. Hunter turned and brought his elbow up into his throat before powering a hard punch into his jaw and knocking him over the side of the temple.

Hunter's assailant scrambled for his knife and slashed it hard through the air, missing his throat by a few short inches. Instinct drove Hunter back on his heels. He lost his balance and fell down on his backside. He went rolling to the side and leaping back up onto his feet in seconds.

The other man lunged towards him, but it was Hunter's turn now. As his assailant charged into him with a bloodcurdling scream, Hunter thrust his blade forward and buried it deep in his stomach. He didn't have to pull the blade out; the man slid off it and crashed down onto the sandy ground, blood bubbling up from his mouth and a look of terrified fear on his face. The other man turned on his heel and ran.

Hunter didn't wait for the other man to die. Death was inevitable. Instead, he turned away and ran over to Quinn on the other side of the temple, but several steps below. He'd heard her cry out when he was fighting the man he'd just killed and had seen her struggling with one of the Illuminati Disciples, but no one else was around to help her. Amy and Lewis were fighting other Disciples in the jungle, and Blanco, Jodie, and Hanna were trying to drive Bauer away from the fountain with a fusillade of gunfire and were unable to hear Quinn's screams.

Hunter leaped down the chunky stone steps two risers at a time until he reached the Disciple attacking the young goth. She was in her thirties and fit and strong. She had just delivered a mighty backhand slap to Quinn's right cheek and knocked her to the ground when Hunter grabbed her shoulder and spun her around.

'I don't normally hit women,' he said. 'But in your case, I'll make an exception.'

She brought her fist and curled it into a tiger punch ready to strike him, but it was too late. Hunter powered his fist into her stomach and blasted the wind out of her. As she doubled over, gasping and straining for air, he looked at Quinn.

'All right?'

'Not yet.' She kicked the woman hard in the face and knocked her out cold. As her body tumbled down onto the ground, Quinn looked at Hunter. 'Now I'm all right.'

'Good stuff.'

Then, the Illuminati chopper rotated in the air one more time and landed, this time at the base of the pyramid. The door swung open to reveal Pedro Razquin. The religious garments he had worn without authority or right were gone, and instead, he was in a plain black suit, shirt, and tie. He adjusted the tie as he strolled over to them, as cool as ice.

'Razquin.' Amy's voice dripped with contempt.

'De Gama's manuscript, now.'

'You already have the Golden One.'

'Perhaps the manuscript has another value to us. Hand it over. Now.'

She obeyed. 'You were with us the whole time, weren't you? Even down at the *Titanic*. We saw you down there, hiding against the hull. We saw you on our sonar. It wasn't just Creed down there.'

'You are mistaken,' the Illuminati leader said coldly. 'We have never been down to the wreck of the *Titanic*. We simply waited and tracked your transponder.'

'But if it wasn't you or the Creed, then who?' Amy asked.

'Not my concern.'

He turned and walked back to the helicopter, manuscript under his arm. When he was inside, the blades began to whir faster as they spooled up ready for flight.

'They're going to kill us all,' Amy said. 'We have nowhere to run, and no guns.'

Then, they heard a bird calling out in the tropical dawn, a strange, haunting cry.

'That is one weird birdcall,' Quinn said.

'It's not a bird,' said Amy, cocking her head to hear more clearly. 'Listen again, carefully.'

They heard it again. A whistle. A man whistling. Then they saw him, and moments later behind him, there were others. A small number of dishevelled men and women dressed in simple wool and cotton tunics. Their jewellery was simple but beautiful, with both the women and the men wearing earrings fashioned from gold or *tumbaga*, an alloy of gold and copper, and one wore some kind of *narigueras*, or nose-ring, crafted with exquisite filigree, now glinting in the rising sun. Others had intricate drawings of animals and ancient gods on their bodies and arms, most likely created with a blend of charcoal and a natural dye obtained from the bright red fruit of the achiote plant. Their tan skin and clear eyes spoke of a hard but healthy life spent mostly outdoors. Hunter was already perplexed, but trying to form an explanation for what he was seeing.

A leader emerged at the head of them, a taller man with a silver beard who was beckoning them with his hand. The clothes he wore differed from the others, with a more refined linen shirt casually unbuttoned and flapping the breeze, and what looked like what might have been vermillion velvet trunk hose below the waist. Then he beckoned them again, and this time called out in Spanish.

'*Venga! Rápido! Por aquí!*'

With the threat of Razquin's heavily armed helicopter rising above them all, Hunter made a rapid assessment of what was going on. The strange newcomers to the scene had come from nowhere, and he guessed they had been observing the battle with the Creed and later the Illuminati from the safety of some hidden quarter of the city. They moved closer cautiously and showed no sign of being a threat. Years of facing peril in some of most dangerous places in the world had helped fine-tune Hunter's instinct, but right now those alarm bells were not ringing. If anything, he was sure these people were good and trying to help them. 'Strange, but I don't think they're hostile.'

'Maybe, maybe not, but who the good goddam hell are they?' Jodie asked, wiping sweat and grime from her forehead.

The leader in the linen shirt spoke again, this time more hurried. '*Si quiere vivir, debe venir con nosotros!*'

'Spanish,' Hanna said. 'Anyone speak Spanish?'

'A little,' Hunter said.

'I can't, but I can speak hand signals,' Jodie said. 'And I know those dudes are trying to help us and the dudes behind us are trying to kill us. You can wait for Hunter's translation, but I'll see you guys later.'

She made off down the steps, turning to grab Quinn's hand. 'C'mon, Quinn. We're outta here.'

'Hey!' Amy said. 'I'm the maternal figure around here, dammit!'

Jodie shrugged. 'Use it or lose it, Mom.'

'I'm following the young rebel,' Lewis said.

'Fine,' Amy said. 'Let's go see what the cast of Gilligan's Island can do to get us out of this mess. If they're cannibals, it's on you, Agent Priest.'

The old man waggled a tanned, bony finger. '*Sólo hablo español. Sólo hablamos español y chibcha.*'

As the man spoke, Hunter translated as best he could. 'I think he's saying they only speak Spanish and Chibcha. He says those are very bad men and he fears he will now lose the Golden One. He says we fought well trying to defend it, which is why he saved our lives.'

Up ahead, the Illuminati chopper was making its third circle of the city in search of them, but they were nowhere to be seen.

The man spoke in Spanish again.

'He says they will not find us in here,' Hunter said. 'The magic bends the light.'

They followed the man with the beard deeper into the safety of the city's invisible heart. Hunter had little fear of their saviours, but he noticed Jodie was clearly still having some trust issues and continued to grip her gun. With more than a few questions on his mind, Hunter went to talk to the bearded man, the one who appeared to be some sort of leader, but just as he caught his eyes, Jodie tugged at his elbow and he turned to face her.

'What's up?' he asked.

'Looks like we made a new enemy today, Hunter,' she said, staring up at the chopper still circling in the hot blue sky. 'One even more powerful and influential than the Creed.'

'I think you might be right,' Hunter said.

'I'm always right, Hunter,' she said with a wink.

'We're going to need to get some kind of protection force down here fast,' Amy said, surveying their new discovery with a mix of pride and anxiety. 'Just like we did with Atlantis. We can never risk the elixir of eternal life falling into the wrong hands. This place needs some serious safeguarding.'

'USG or UNESCO?' Lewis asked, smiling as the Delta team slung their packs over their shoulders and got ready to move out.

'Both,' Hunter and Amy said at the same time. Above them, the helicopter slowly disappeared. They were alone at last. Now it was time to find out a little more about the mysterious band of strangers who had saved their lives, but when Amy turned to thank the man with the beard, he and his small group of strange followers had all vanished from sight. 'Would you look at that? They've all gone.'

Hunter turned and scanned the jungle. 'Very odd.'

'Who do you think they were?' Quinn asked.

Blanco clapped an arm around her shoulder and wheeled her towards the path and a long hike back to their Jeeps. 'You know what, Q? I think we can talk about that later when we get back to the hotel. After a shower and a beer, in that order, yeah?'

'In that order,' she said with a smile.

40

When Amy Fox woke, the first thing she registered was warm but weak sunlight on her eyelids. Then she realised the ship had finally stopped rolling on the waves. Calm for the first time since their chopper had landed out on the *Ostøya* last night. She opened her eyes and enjoyed the small round patch of blue sky she was able to see through the porthole at the foot of her bunk. Calm and clear.

She checked her watch on the small bedside table and saw it was already mid-morning. A full day since the battle back in the jungle. Pulling herself up on her elbows, she rested her back against the headboard and winced when she saw her filthy dirt-stained clothes hanging over the edge of the chair where she had dumped them last night before crawling into bed. And her arms and legs, all covered in cuts and bruises, hurt like hell too.

And where was Hunter?

Not next to her, where he had most certainly been when she'd fallen asleep last night. He was gone, and so were his clothes. She blinked in the morning light and swung her legs out of bed, yawned, and stretched her arms. The ship rolled slightly, just for long enough to remind her that she was not on dry land, and then was steady again. She knew enough about ships to know that anything as big as Skulberg's *Ostøya* was mostly stable on the high seas, barring some of the more powerful storms.

She dressed and splashed cold water on her face from the small basin beside her bunk, drying herself with the little towel folded over a small metal bar. All very nautical, she thought. Still, it was good of Skulberg to think of it. Now, she left her cabin and made her way along the corridor until she reached the nearest outside door. She stepped out onto the portside deck on the shady side of the ship and shivered. Sea air was mostly cold air, especially this far north.

Making her way along the deck to the stern and turning, she felt the sun on her face once again and smiled. The gentle warmth felt good. It relaxed her and she soon felt the tension bleed away from her neck and shoulders. By the time she crossed the stern and made her way up the starboard side of the ship, she felt almost human again. All she needed now was a good, strong cup of coffee and life would be okay again.

Up ahead, she found Hunter. He was standing in a small huddle of sailors, along with Hanna Vikander, Blanco, and the rest of the HARPA team. They were all facing Skulberg as the old Norwegian naval officer held court like a renaissance king. As she approached, Hunter turned and smiled.

'I see you're more of an owl than a lark.'

'Coffee,' she said. 'Need and want morning coffee.'

'Morning coffee? We're halfway to lunch.'

'Need and want coffee. Do not care about trivialities like time.'

When her coffee arrived, Amy took a long, deep sip. 'That's better. Now, exactly why were we summoned out here, Olav?'

'To witness Operation Njord,' Skulberg said. 'Nearly forty years in the making!'

Amy frowned. 'I don't understand.'

'You ask why I brought you out to the *Ostøya* last night,' Skulberg began. 'You ask what it is I wanted to show you, out in this wide expanse of empty ocean. You also are wondering who else was down at the ship's wreck when you were there, fighting with the Creed. Well, now all of those questions will be answered. You see, it was my men your sonar saw down at the wreck, quietly employed fitting AI nanopillows to the *Titanic*'s hull.'

Amy was astonished. 'What the hell?'

Skulberg laughed. 'Now, please, Agent Fox, Dr Hunter, and the rest of Team HARPA, watch carefully over there to the ship's south.'

Skulberg swept his hand out over the ship's rail and smiled. With his other hand, he brought a two-way radio up to his mouth and spoke in English. 'Okay, go ahead. We're ready.'

The other sailors left the huddle, each one making his or her own way to a section of the railing where they stopped and stared out to sea.

Silence.

'What's going on?' Jodie asked. 'Because it kinda seems like whatever he thought was going to happen kinda did not happen.'

'Right,' Quinn said. 'I feel kind of bad for him, what with his big surprise falling on its ass like that.'

Skulberg said nothing.

The radio in his hand crackled back, a voice coming through the static. 'It's done. All looking good, sir.'

Blanco turned to Hunter, brow furrowed and voice a low, gravelly whisper. 'Are you thinking what I'm thinking, Max?'

Hunter felt a shiver go up his spine and neck. 'I don't want to think it in case I jinx it.'

Blanco shrugged. 'I can think it because I know I ain't got that sort of power.'

Amy glanced at Hunter. 'What are you two talking... Oh my God! You can't mean...'

Skulberg raised a pair of small field glasses to his eyes and stared out across the sea. 'Soon, very soon. Nothing can stop this now. There! I see it!'

Amy followed his line of vision and saw nothing. Then she saw something. A ripple of excitement moved along the line of sailors. Skulberg tightened his jaw, nodded his head as if in reply to someone's question. Overcome with emotion, he masked his eyes behind the binoculars.

A couple of hundred yards away from the *Ostøya*, the surface of the sea was foaming and bubbling and breaking apart. A deep shadow darkened the water just below the surface as more white bubbles popped and spewed and rolled on the waves. Then, Amy saw something metallic poke up through the water. Dark, rusted and gnarled, and covered in the dark orange rusticles she had seen when they dived down earlier to the *Titanic*.

'My God, it's true,' she whispered. 'You're actually raising the *Titanic*! But why?'

Skulberg lowered the binoculars. 'Why raise it? Because its condition has deteriorated so much over the past few years. If we want to bring her to the surface, it's now or never. In less than thirty years, she'll be gone completely. She's fragile enough as it is. Only today's brand-new technology makes such a dream technically feasible. Using AI, we were able to inflate thousands of separate balloons at just the right time and place, constantly inflating and deflating to ensure total stability as we lifted the wreck to the surface. Keeping the fragile hull on these giant, ever-changing cushions is the only way to make this happen.'

'I'm astonished. But if you were planning on raising her yourself, why ask us to get the idol?'

'I did not ask you to get the idol. I asked you to get the compass and the ring. Retrieving these from the Creed was out of my reach. I needed your help. I knew you would be able to get the rest of de Gama's relics using your unique skills. What I did not know was that you would be able to find a way down to the wreck on your own. That was very resourceful. Besides, my real desire was to obtain the *Titanic*, not the relics. I have no interest in whatever de Gama was after in the jungle. All I wanted was my family's property back.'

'And the *Titanic*,' she said.

'And the *Titanic*,' he said with a wicked smile.

'Well, it's still an astonishing achievement.'

'Indeed.' Skulberg returned the glasses to his eyes, utterly absorbed in the historical salvage operation he had spent so many years funding and organising. It was the crowning glory to his entire long and successful career and his attention was transfixed on every single second of it.

'This can't be happening,' Blanco said. 'Damn.'

Quinn was pretending not to care but had already taken dozens of photos with her phone.

Behind her, Jodie couldn't conceal her amazement. 'This is the most incredible thing I ever saw...'

'And she's seen Atlantis,' Hunter said. 'Seriously.'

The upper sections of the Edwardian ocean liner's bow section were more visible now, covered in salty seawater and dimly reflecting the sun in the occasional sparkle or flash. The bridge was almost completely above the surface, as were the officer's quarters just behind it.

'Is that the Marconi room?' Skulberg said, his voice frail and filled with emotion.

'I think so, sir,' said a sailor. 'But it's hard to tell because of the rusticles. Everything is so obscured and distorted.'

Rising further from the depths, they all saw the main front mast, complete with a smashed, crumpled crow's nest. It was lying flat over the front part of the ship where it had broken away and fallen down on the night she'd gone down. The sight was eerie and sombre and its gravity was lost on no one.

Amy almost felt dizzy with the impact of what she had just witnessed. 'I'm impressed, Admiral. I have to say, very impressed.'

The old Norwegian sailor beside her smiled and opened a small metal watch. 'And we're bang on time, too.'

Inside the antique pocket watch, Amy saw a tiny portrait. 'Wait a minute, that's a painting of Francisco de Gama?' Amy asked.

Skulberg looked confused. 'Of course, why would you doubt it? This was once his watch, dating from the sixteenth century.'

'Er... Max. Get over here, now.'

The English archaeologist approached with his usual gentlemanly stroll, one hand casually tucked into his pocket. He gave Skulberg a nod and smiled at Amy. 'Which of my many skills is required now?'

She frowned at him and handed him the small portrait miniature Skulberg had just shown her. 'Does this remind you, or your colossal ego, of anyone?'

He ignored her barb and looked at the tiny picture. 'No.'

'Where did you get it?' Lewis asked.

'Olav just handed it to me. It was inside his old pocket watch – de Gama's, in fact. He said it was from the 1500s. I didn't know they made mechanical watches that early.'

'Sure they did,' Lewis said. 'German watchmaker Peter Henlein invented the first pocket watch in 1510. His miniaturisation of mainsprings allowed him to make ever-smaller timepieces and... Sorry.'

Amy smiled. 'Thanks, Lewis. But back to the portrait that was inside it. Look closer, please.'

'It's just a well-manicured gent from a few hundred years ago,' said Hunter, growing bored.

'Now, ignore the clothes and imagine longer hair.'

Behind him, Jodie gasped. 'Holy crap, that's the dude who helped us out of the garden!'

'You can't be serious?' Blanco asked.

'Sure, I am,' she said. 'It's the guy with the beard and the linen shirt! He has exactly the same face!'

'That's quite impossible,' Skulberg said. 'Because as I say, this is a portrait of Francisco de Gama. One made much later in his life than the one you likely saw from the exhibition. Here he had a beard and much less hair up top. There is no way you saw this man in the jungle because he died nearly five hundred years ago.'

Lewis shook his head, full of doubt. 'He's right. It doesn't look much like the young dude we saw in the oil painting back in Jim's office.'

'That was when he was a much younger man. This portrait must have been taken when he was older. It looks just like him,' Amy said.

'They're identical,' said Jodie. 'You think he took some of the elixir? You think he's been living down there for five hundred years?'

Blanco and Lewis looked more closely at the picture.

'Looks nothing like him,' Blanco said, turning away and looking back at the *Titanic*.

'I don't know.' Lewis peered in close and took a much longer look. 'I think Jodie's right, after all. It's absolutely identical, and it's his watch, too! I think it's the same guy.'

His mind buzzing with the prospect of de Gama living for nearly half a millennium down in some of the most remote jungle on the planet, Hunter laughed, but his smile soon faded when he took another look at the portrait. 'It couldn't be, could it?'

* * *

MORE FROM ROB JONES

Another book from Rob Jones, *The Excalibur Code*, is available to order now here:

https://mybook.to/ExcaliburCodeBackAd

ABOUT THE AUTHOR

Rob Jones has published over forty books in the genres of action-adventure, action-thriller and crime. Many of his chart-topping titles have enjoyed number-one rankings and his Joe Hawke and Jed Mason series have been international bestsellers. Originally from England, today he lives in Australia with his wife and children.

Sign up to Rob's mailing list for news, competitions and updates on future books.

Follow Rob on social media here:

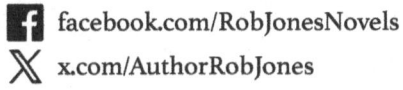

facebook.com/RobJonesNovels
x.com/AuthorRobJones

ALSO BY ROB JONES

The Hunter Files
The Atlantis Covenant
The Revelation Relic
The Titanic Legacy
The Excalibur Code

THE Hit LIST

Every crime has a story...

THE HIT LIST IS A NEWSLETTER DEDICATED TO PULSE-POUNDING, HIGH-OCTANE ACTION THRILLERS!

SIGN UP TO MAKE SURE YOU'RE ON OUR HIT LIST FOR EXCLUSIVE DEALS, AUTHOR CONTENT, AND COMPETITIONS.

SIGN UP TO OUR NEWSLETTER

BIT.LY/THEHITLISTNEWS

Boldwood

Boldwood Books is an award-winning fiction publishing company seeking out the best stories from around the world.

Find out more at www.boldwoodbooks.com

Join our reader community for brilliant books, competitions and offers!

Follow us
@BoldwoodBooks
@TheBoldBookClub

Sign up to our weekly deals newsletter

https://bit.ly/BoldwoodBNewsletter

www.ingramcontent.com/pod-product-compliance
Lightning Source LLC
Chambersburg PA
CBHW011949150426
43194CB00018B/2850